Readers Rave About Star Sisterz™

"Told with a lot of humor and teen angst."

—*School Library Journal*

"Exactly what a series read should be—fun and fast-paced . . ."

—Kidsreads.com

"Parents will approve, and girls likely will love them."

—*Salem Statesman Journal*

"Tween readers will . . . cheer Nova on as she seeks the courage to be herself."

—*St. Louis Post-Dispatch*

"A book girls will not want to put down."

—Bookloons.com

"The situations Nova finds herself in are ones everyone can identify with, and I found myself rooting for her all the way."

—Michele Ivy Davis, author of *Evangeline Brown and the Cadillac Motel*

"A fresh, hip and charming tale that is laugh-out-loud funny, while at the same time a reminder to us all to follow our passion! Nova definitely rocks."

—Elizabeth Cody Kimmel, author of *Lily B. on the Brink of Cool*

Nova and the Charmed Three

Tea Emesse

MIRROR
STONE

NOVA AND THE CHARMED THREE

Cover art by Taia Morley
Interior art by A. Friend
First Printing: February 2006
Library of Congress Catalog Card Number: 2005928117

9 8 7 6 5 4 3 2 1

ISBN-10: 0-7869-3991-5
ISBN-13: 978-0-7869-3991-6
620-95473740-001-EN

U.S., CANADA,
ASIA, PACIFIC, & LATIN AMERICA
Wizards of the Coast, Inc.
P.O. Box 707
Renton, WA 98057-0707
+1-800-324-6496

EUROPEAN HEADQUARTERS
Hasbro UK Ltd
Caswell Way
Newport, Gwent NP9 0YH
GREAT BRITAIN
Please keep this address for your records

Visit our website at www.mirrorstonebooks.com

With love to my brilliant and beautiful
Warner Star Sisterz: Gabriella, Flannery,
Leia, and Victoria.
Long may you sparkle and shine!

Chapter 1

I should have been so happy. Let me count the ways:

1. I'd been a ninth-grader at Middletown High for a while, and despite my agonizing fears beforehand, it was pretty cool.

2. Mom totally accepted my choice to drop ballet. (She actually began taking ballet lessons herself.)

3. Dad was so stoked about my guitar that he sometimes even played my guitar, Roxie, by himself.

But most of all:

4. Joe Tsai—my dream man—had been giving me guitar lessons for two glorious months. Ah, Joe Tsai! Let me say it just one more time: Joe Tsai. Joe often said I was a natural, that I was born with talent, etc. And we always had a blast at my lessons.

What more could a music-loving, guitar-riffing girl want in her life? I was pretty much over the moon with joy.

And then, just a few weeks ago, something even more incredible happened.

It all started right after school. I'd been looking forward to my guitar lesson all day (and not just the "scenery," otherwise known as Joe.)

I walked into Joe's garage—and he didn't even say "hi." He just stared at the floor.

Joe's garage is huge, especially compared to his house. It's all shingled on the outside and isn't attached to his house, like maybe they'd built it as an afterthought. The yard between the house and the garage is all lush and green, with tons of enormous tropical-looking plants.

Even though it was afternoon when I got to my lesson, it was damp and chilly in that garage. As usual, I was shivering, but not from the cold. I was always nervous and excited and all shook up until I got into my music. Then I'd forget about myself.

I snuck a quick peek at Joe, who seemed to be glaring at his cell phone. Okay. He was sitting on the stage at the far end of the garage, which is where we do our thang. There's a drum set up there, a keyboard stuck off to the side, and some amps and stuff, with big snarls of wire everywhere.

On the far wall, near the door to the house, are shelves with plastic bins for recyclables. They're always overflowing with magazines and newspapers. Beyond them is a bit of clutter consisting of those kinds of things people hang on to "just in case": a dusty, folded up mesh playpen, an easel-type blackboard with chalk in the tray, a drafting table, cheap plastic chairs, and an old red metal wagon. Six brightly colored fabric kites hang from the rafters. The garage smells clean, like wood shavings.

I walked over to the stage, where Joe was sitting, took my beloved Roxie out of her case, and tuned her.

Joe didn't even notice when I started singing "Three Blind Mice," instead of the tune we had been working on.

Finally, I quit playing. "Joe! Hello?"

He looked at me.

"Uh," I said. "I'm here for my lesson? In fact, I'm teaching myself here!"

When Joe didn't even smile at my little joke, I got serious. "Joe, is everything okay?"

Joe snapped to attention. "Huh? Oh . . . sorry, Nova. I guess I'm just bummed out. Roast Beef called right before you came over to say his mom is making him quit our band. He's the lead singer! I just gave Ivy the word that we're totally sunk." Joe put his face in his hands.

"Ivy? Who's Ivy?"

Joe looked up. "You know, my drummer."

For some reason, that "my" bothered me. "Oh."

Joe flashed his so-white teeth at me in one of his amazing smiles. "Well, whatever. I mean, we're in a bad spot, but that shouldn't affect your lesson. Why don't you play that chord pattern we worked on last week? Then play the whole song, if you feel comfortable."

I did the exercises, and then ran through my song, losing myself in the lyrics. Luckily, I had never been self-conscious about my singing in front of Joe. (My hair? A totally different story!)

When I reached the end of my song, Joe sat there staring at me. Just staring. Finally, he jumped up. "Why didn't I think of it before?"

"Huh?"

What was he talking about?

Joe took me by my shoulders. My heart palpitated. I looked down at my chest just to be sure my heart wasn't actually visible.

"Please say you'll do it," Joe said.

✵ **4** ✵

"Do what?"

Run away with you? Be yours for eternity?

"Join Ivy and me! Become our lead singer! Take Roast Beef's place!" Joe's voice got a little bit louder with each phrase.

I laughed. "Me? No way."

Joe was pacing now. "Nova, you'll love it! Just wait until you meet Ivy. She's tiny, but what a drummer. You'll totally dig working with her."

"Well, I . . . uh," I mumbled.

Joe snapped his fingers. "In fact, our practices start right after your lesson. If you stick around, you can meet Ivy, and we can do some tunes together . . . see how it goes. Please, Nova? What do you say?"

I was pretty sure Joe was just desperate. "I don't know . . . I know you're stuck without . . . uh, Lunch Meat, but—"

"Roast Beef," Joe said. "His name is Roast Beef."

I shrugged. "I mean, it's your band. Don't *you* want to be the lead singer?"

"Me? I'm strictly the backup guy," Joe said. His teeth flashed white. Just a tiny bit crooked, yet extremely attractive. "You are our new singer—you just don't know it yet. But I do."

Wow. Who could argue with that?

I smiled. "Okay! I'll do it! But . . . " I hesitated. I felt kind of stupid even saying it aloud. "I have to call my mom and tell her to come pick me up later."

"No prob!" Joe handed me his cell phone. "Here, you can use this. Tell her you'll be ready around six." (Sigh. Joe is *so* understanding!)

I dialed the ballet studio where Mom was taking lessons. (Yes, I knew the number from heart since I'd spent way too much time there in my past life.)

"Oh, exciting!" Mom said after I explained. "Six is no problem. I can stay here and work on my pirouettes until then."

As soon as Mom said the word "exciting," I went lightheaded with joy. I mean—come on! Joe WANTED ME for his garage band. Wow—a billion times over.

I felt like I should be looking around for my fairy godmother. She must be hanging around up in the rafters above all those bright kites. Were all my dreams going to come true, right then and right there?

Don't forget to make Joe love me forever, I wished silently, just in case.

Chapter 2

I was handing Joe's phone back to him, noticing that our hands touched briefly (oooh!) when he looked toward the door.

"There you are!" he said, smiling. "And I've got some great news!"

A tiny person stood in the doorway. She was just a shadowy silhouette with the late afternoon sunshine falling behind her.

I smiled toward the door and waved, trying to act cool although my stomach was tied up in knots from excitement. She paused there another moment, and then stepped quickly through the doorway. As she walked toward us, I checked her out: Small, like I said. Silvery pale blonde hair, very sleek and shiny, cut short. Big almond-shaped, slightly tilted turquoise eyes—which were watching me.

Cat, I thought. *Total Siamese kitten. And playful, fun, and funny, I'll bet. She'll be a total blast to know.*

"Hey, Joe," she said, in a throaty voice. "What's up? Did Roast Beef decide he couldn't leave us after all?"

"No, the Beef is gone for good," Joe said. "But it's all good. You'll see."

I sucked in a big shaky breath, realizing I'd been neglecting to breathe. No wonder. I felt not only thrilled but also breathless. Okay, I felt a little less thrilled and a little less breathless when I saw Joe bend down and start kind of whispering in this person's ear. When I saw how she looked way up at him, in a "you're such a big man and I'm such a tiny delicate female" kind of a way.

It was a bit off-putting. Still, Joe said she was cool. If he liked her, I'd like her.

"This is Nova," Joe said. "Our new lead singer."

I put my hand out. Ivy put her hands on her dinky hips and stared at me.

Well, I never know about that handshaking thing anyway. Maybe it just wasn't cool. I shrugged and slipped my hands into my jeans pockets.

"Nice to meet you, New Girl," Ivy said.

I laughed.

She didn't.

"Uh," I said. "Well. Nice to meet you. It's Nova, by the way."

"Wait'll you hear Nova sing, Ivy," Joe said. "She's amazing."

"Amazing, huh?" Ivy said. "We'll see about that."

Okay, so this wasn't going exactly as well as I had hoped.

Was it my imagination, or had Ivy actually just sneered at me? Actually, I'd never seen anyone "sneer" before—so probably not. Maybe she was in a bad mood for something not having to do with me at all. Or maybe she was one of those people who is just deadly honest. You've got to learn to deal with these types without having your ego crushed every time they say something.

And, hey. Even if the drummer was a tad on the blunt side, things were definitely not all bad, right?

Right. I did a quick recap of my big picture: Joe's garage band (me!!!), no ballet, being able to practice on Roxie any time, anywhere, at home. Life was good.

I smiled at Ivy. *We will be friends,* I thought, willing it to be true. *I'll get used to your ways. You'll learn to appreciate me. We'll bond through our music.*

"Come on, guys, let's get started," Joe said. "Why don't we kick off with something easy?"

After Joe started us off on the first song ("Do You

Believe in Magic"), I warmed right up. In fact, I was dripping sweat as I joined my sounds to his.

(Note to self: layer clothing when playing with band!)

We'd been practicing this song in my lesson, so I already knew all the chords and lyrics. But the pure pulsating energy in a group is so unbelievably different from strumming away by yourself. You can't help but jump and dance and hop.

I was totally grooving out on the song, until I turned around and caught a glimpse of Joe. There he was, smiling his perfect smile, strumming his bass, and cuddling up with Ivy. (So, okay, he wasn't actually touching her, but he was leaning as close as he could get without contact). Ivy gazed up at him as she tapped out the beat on her drums.

Ivy looked over and caught me staring. She gave me this weird little tight-lipped smile and leaned closer to Joe.

Have you ever seen a kitten when someone dangles catnip in front of her? Right before she jumps? Yep. All smiling and purring, slicking back her fur. That was definitely the vibe.

After that, well, I kind of lost my edge, and that's an understatement.

Ivy tapped out the last few beats of "Do You Believe in Magic" on her bass drum, and then hit the cymbals for the grand finale.

For a second, we just listened to the crash of the cymbals echoing in Joe's giant garage.

Ivy was the first to speak. "Uh, sorry to be the one to break it to you, New Girl, but I've gotta be honest. Roast Beef did that song WAY better."

"Yeah, he did," Joe said.

My heart sank. My eyes stung. I swallowed, hard. I knew I'd blown it, but hearing it out loud (especially from Joe) hurt. So much for being thrilled. It was all over. I wasn't going to be a member of the garage band for long. I'd been discovered for the fraud I was.

I opened my mouth to apologize, but Joe cut me off. "But we don't expect any different from a first gig, do we Ivy?"

Ivy rapped out a rat-a-tat-tat and then whacked the cymbals again. Joe didn't seem to notice that she had said nothing. But I did.

Joe smiled at me. "You'll get it. It just takes a while to get the feel for the group, you know? No worries, Nova!"

I adore Joe.

"I'm going to run into the house for a minute," Joe said. "Do either of you need anything?"

I shook my head. "No, thanks."

Ivy said, "Do you have any root beer?"

"I think so," Joe said. "Organic, right?"

She smiled, her eyes flicking toward me to be sure I understood they were so tight that Joe knew her preferences in sodas.

Then they said, together, "Lots of ice in the glass." They burst out laughing. I forced a smile.

After Joe left, Ivy turned to me and giggled. "Ooooh. I just love having cute guys wait on me, don't you?"

My jaw dropped. How crass. How classless. And even worse if all cute guys acted like Joe—so willing to wait on someone so manipulative.

And then she said, "Joe loves it when I order him around. It makes him feel manly and powerful."

Oh, ugh.

Not to be shallow or anything (okay, I knew I was being shallow but I can't help it every once in a while), but right at that moment, even just looking at Ivy bugged me. She was such a tiny, graceful, sleek Siamese cat that next to her I felt like a huge bumbling shaggy golden retriever. I couldn't help comparing. Even though I kept telling myself to get a grip. But worse yet was what she'd just said.

Maybe she was just joking around. Maybe she has a very weird sense of humor and was just trying to see how I'd react.

After that, it got very quiet in the garage. Ivy sat at her drums, patting them softly with the drumsticks. Not looking at me. Which was just as well. It's not like I really wanted to chitchat with her anyway. At least until she got out of the bizarre mood she seemed to be in.

I looked around for something, anything, to do. Hmm. There were the Tsais' recycling bins. I snatched up the newspaper on the top of the pile, and started thumbing through it.

My eyes settled on a headline: "Band Idol Competition." The more I read, the more excited I felt.

I blurted out, "Ivy! Did you know that Band Idol is coming to Middletown?"

Ivy looked up. "Really? Here?"

"Yes! They're having tryouts next month! This is so cool. I love that show!" My voice squeaked a little bit, I was so stoked.

"Not that that has anything to do with us"—especially you, she insinuated with her voice—"but why don't you read it to me?"

Who died and made me your servant?

I faked a smile. My mom says if you fake-smile, you start to feel happy.

(Note to Mom: that little theory just didn't feel like it was working right then.)

"It's kind of long. You can read it when I'm done." I looked back down at the newspaper, glancing over the particulars. My heart was pounding like crazy. This looked big.

Ivy sprang up and trotted over to me. "But why can't you just read it to me?" Our eyes met. Hers widened. "Please, Nova?"

Hmm. Interesting. She seemed to have total recall of my name when she wanted something from me. Maybe her bad attitude was some odd form of shyness. Maybe Ivy was just terrible with new people. Maybe someday we'd actually be best of friends. After all, everyone was entitled to an off day, right?

I tried to ignore that little voice inside, the one saying, "Right. And maybe the world actually is shaped like a Frisbee."

I sighed and began reading the article out loud. "Local bands could be discovered big time when Band Idol starts tryouts . . ."

"Did you say Band Idol?" Joe's voice came from the door to the house. He entered the garage juggling some drinks and a bag of tortilla chips. I couldn't help noticing that he was looking incredibly hunky is his grayish-green hoodie and black jeans. "They're having local tryouts? You guys! This could be our big break."

I felt happiness rising inside my chest like a great big bubble.

"If New Girl can ever get her act together," Ivy said.

My bubble popped.

I looked at Joe, who was smiling in an "Ivy's so adorable when she jokes" kind of a way.

How come guys are so oblivious?

Joe gave Ivy her root beer. He took a swig of his own soda and plunked down on the edge of the stage. "Nova, read the story!" He was obviously stoked. "Start at the very beginning!"

Now, Joe asking me to read was a different story! I gladly picked up the paper and started to read the article about the band competition out loud again, from the beginning. My breath caught as I read. They'd start with local tryouts. Winners of those would actually play on the television show—in Hawaii. The grand prize winners would get a recording contract, and tons of exposure.

My mouth hung open (I was trying not to drool) and I was panting like I'd just run a mile.

"Meow?" Ivy said. (Okay, so she actually said, "Joe?")

I looked up.

"Joe, what do you think?" Ivy rattled the ice in her glass and rat-a-tat-tatted with her fingers on the floor. Uh, can you say, annoying? The girl was just a bundle of nervous, wiry energy.

Joe said, "I think this could be big for us. Seriously. What do you guys think?"

I opened my mouth, and Ivy and I said in stereo sound: "Very cool!"

We all laughed. Unfortunately, I choked.

Great. Choking on my own spit. Way to impress Joe.

Joe thumped me on the back as I coughed helplessly. "Are you okay?"

"Sorry," I gasped.

"You and my little sister," Joe said.

Urk. I absolutely detest it when he compares me to his little sister. I'm a woman, for crying out loud! Well, kind of, anyway.

Ivy looked over at Joe, all huge turquoise slanted eyes and gleaming white fur—I mean "hair." I waited for her to climb onto his shoulder and rub her face against his, but instead she said, "If *you* think we can pull it together for the competition, I'm sure we can."

Oh. Brother.

Joe turned to me. "Are you up for it, Nova?"

"Well, at the very least, it gives us a target to shoot for."

Joe's face fell a little bit.

I couldn't take it.

"I'm sure we'll be competition-worthy by then!" I said. Actually, I was enthused about the competition, but Ivy's reaction had taken the wind out of my sails. Which is ridiculous, I'll admit. I resolved to cut it out, and be genuine no matter how fake I personally found Ivy.

Joe said, "The White Shirts were discovered in a talent contest—did you guys know that?"

"No kidding?" I blurted. I totally love the White Shirts!

Joe nodded and started rooting around in a pile of music mags. "Let me see, let me see," he muttered. "I just read an article where they interviewed them . . . Here it is."

And then, you won't believe it. Or maybe you will.

Ivy said, "Joe, would you mind reading it to us?" She barked a short laugh.

I held my breath. If he said no, maybe he wasn't as at Ivy's beck and call as she seemed to think he was. *Say no. Say no.*

"Sure, Ivy!" he said. And then he did.

Ivy looked pointedly at me, as if to say, "See? He *loves* me."

And maybe he did. Then again—surely not. Surely Joe was smart enough to see through Ivy's scams.

Joe finished reading and gave us the thumbs up.

"Yeah!" I said. "We're next!"

Ivy yawned and stretched. She glanced at the oversized pink plastic watch on her wrist. "Hey, I've gotta run."

She went up to Joe—close. Hadn't she ever heard about personal space? I guess not. She looked deep into his eyes. "Bye, Joe." She took his hand. Wow, I was starting to feel really uncomfortable. She flashed me a look. Did she *want* me to feel uncomfortable? "See you later at the library?"

"Sounds good," Joe said.

Ivy did this "cute" little thing where she walked backward out of the garage, waving the whole time. To Joe, of course. Not to "New Girl."

When she was gone, Joe started flipping through the magazine again. It was quiet in the garage. I should say something. We should be talking.

I halfway hoped Mom would hurry to pick me up.

Hey, did I mind hanging out with Joe? Not on your life. But I just felt so awkward. I was frantically trying to think of something to say. I couldn't think of one thing.

"So how does it feel to be Ivy's slave?" I asked.

Oh, no! Had I just said that? Evidently my subconscious had decided to make a joke but my voice didn't sound at all joking! My tone was kind of weird. Actually accusatory or something.

(Note to self: take acting lessons; work on tone.)

Joe shrugged. "Ivy's a little crazy sometimes. But she's really cool once you get to know her. You'll learn to love her like I did."

I gulped and my ears started buzzing. "LOVE"??? Did Joe just say he loved Ivy?

Man.

He smiled, like she was the cutest thing he'd ever seen. Gag. Puke. He shook his head. "She's so funny."

FUNNY? Not exactly the way I would have described that barracuda.

I barely pulled off a polite smile, I was so heartsick. Obviously, Ivy liked Joe. Joe liked Ivy. And I was simply a fill-in for Roast Beef.

Just call me Turkey.

My life was ruined.

Just then I heard a car horn toot outside the garage. Mom. Here, to save the day! Of course, I wished she wasn't driving our ancient beat-up station wagon, but there you go. The Darlings are not big on class.

"Oh, there's my mom! See ya," I said, grabbing Roxie and sticking her tenderly into her case. I was sort of wondering if he'd suggest we meet at the library, too.

But all Joe said was, "You might want to practice those riffs. With a little more work, they'll be totally hot."

It would've been a total letdown, except then he smiled his blindingly adorable smile. And walked me out to the driveway.

Oh, sigh on Joe Tsai (which is actually pronounced "Sigh," just in case you didn't know. How amazingly appropriate is that?) He's the nicest guy in the entire universe.

I climbed into the front seat, moving Mom's bag with her ballet junk onto the floor, and settling Roxie's case on my lap.

"How did it go?" Mom pushed straggling strands back up into her ballerina knot and waved at Joe. He grinned and waved back, which should have sent Mom into a dead faint but didn't seem to faze her in the least. (Which just goes to show moms are not like other people. They're impervious to hotties.)

"Okay for a first time, I guess," I said. "How about you? How was ballet?"

Mom backed down Joe's driveway. "Great! Well, my middle-aged knees are a little shocked at finding themselves back in ballet classes." She shrugged. "Here I thought I was in quite good shape."

"Hey," I said, noticing Mom's glowing face. She looked so much happier, so much more relaxed since she had gone back to taking ballet lessons. Maybe it had been tough all those years, pushing me into doing what she actually yearned to do herself. "You'll get used to it! It just takes some practice, and it will all come back to you."

"I hope so. So, tell me about the band! Who else is in it besides Joe?"

Ugh. Please don't remind me. "Just one other person. She's the drummer. Her name is Ivy and . . . "

I saw Ivy walking along the sidewalk as we approached one of those housing developments where every house looks like a clone of the other. With all that nervous energy of hers, I would have thought she would be clear on the other side of town by now. "There she is now."

"Oh, great," Mom pulled up alongside Ivy. "I get to meet her!"

Please tell me this is not happening.

Chapter 3

Mom rolled her window down. "Yoo hoo!" she cried.

"Yoo hoo"? Who yells "Yoo hoo"? I felt like I was in a cartoon. A very black-humored cartoon. Come to think of it, I felt more like I was in the middle of the worst horror movie in the world.

"I don't think she needs a ride," I hissed.

"Of course she does!" Mom said, all cheery. "Ivy!"

Ivy turned around, frowning a little bit. Finally, she saw me. She waved half-heartedly and trudged over to the car.

"Hop on in!" Mom chirped, like she was a robin instead of a human.

Could she possibly be any cheerier? UGH.

"Well, I . . . " Ivy looked at me.

I spread my hands in a "parents, what can you do?" kind of a gesture.

Ivy shrugged. "Okay." She reached for the door handle.

"Oh, no," Mom said. "Wait a sec. I forgot." She jumped out of the car and opened the back seat door.

Mom? Have you gone totally, absolutely bonkers?

"I forgot I had all these plants in the back. I'm going to put in a little salad garden. Greens are so good for you, you know, and the fresher the better." She quit blathering for the briefest second, long enough for Ivy and me to lock eyes. Ivy actually looked sympathetic. Maybe her mother acted bizarrely at times, too.

"So . . . " Mom opened the back door and started pulling flats of tiny leafy plants out. "Nova? Hop out please. I think we'll put the plants in the front seat, and Ivy and you can snuggle down in the back."

Snuggle down? Does Mom labor under the delusion that we're three years old, and ready for our naps?

I climbed out of the front seat slowly. Before I knew it, Ivy and I were in the backseat. We both blinked. I'm sure my face mirrored Ivy's "What happened? How did I get here?" expression.

Ivy told Mom how to get to her house. It was way out of our way, but of course Mom made it sound like we were dying to drive through town.

There was silence for a few minutes. I thought it was pretty peaceful and nice, but obviously Mom didn't agree because she started asking Ivy one question after the other.

"Do you go to Middletown High or West Valley, Ivy?" (West Valley's the other high school in my town.)

"Actually, I'm home-schooled," Ivy said. "I've been for forever."

"How interesting," was Mom's opinion.

Mine: not so much. But no one cared what I thought, as usual.

"It's such a blast!" Ivy enthused. "My dad is my teacher. Well, I use the word loosely. He's majorly laid-back."

"Oh?" My mom couldn't quite hide her feelings that "laid-back" might not be the best qualification for a teacher.

"Yeah. No sitting in a classroom for me." Ivy sniffed like sitting in a classroom was on a par with having your fingernails ripped from your hand one by one. Hey, school can be a drag—but it's not all that bad!

"We hit the museums, head out for hikes in the woods, go to tons of movie matinees . . . And, of course,

Dad plays lots of instruments, so we play music all the time. And, for math, we cook."

"Does your mom teach you too? Or does she work?"

Ivy swallowed. "No, actually. It's just Dad and me. My mom died when I was a little kid."

Oh, man. I couldn't even imagine it.

"I'm so sorry," Mom said, and I kind of gulped squeaked, "Me, too."

"Thanks," Ivy said quietly. Then she proceeded to rave more about home schooling, like it was held at Disneyland or something. I tuned out, until I heard her saying, "Joe says that's the life—hanging with Dad most of the day, learning by osmosis."

She glanced over at me, and smiled her mean little tight-lipped smile.

Yeah, yeah. I get it.

I could tell from the way Mom was smiling and nodding, glancing into the rearview mirror at Ivy that she was totally digging our little drumming kitty cat. Man, Ivy was turning on the charm for Mom, and I don't mean maybe. And Mom was totally eating it up. So much for being a good judge of character! I had no idea how gullible Mom was.

I tuned out the sound of Ivy's burbling voice and

Mom's heartfelt chuckles, escaping into a daydream of quitting the garage band in order to get away from Ivy. Hey, I hadn't even known the girl twenty-four hours and I was considering dumping my lifelong dream in order to not know her anymore.

But, wait a minute. What was I thinking? I'd sooner chew off my right hand (that's my strumming hand!) than quit Joe's band.

So Joe thought Ivy was totally It. So he let her manipulate him. So maybe Ivy was a really good drummer. (I hated to admit it but it was the truth.) But how could anyone take her attitude? She was all "I'm so helpless and sweet" to Joe, but around me, she was a giant jerk!

Okay. I felt like quitting again.

I took a deep breath and clenched my hands. We stopped at a red light. And I "stopped," too. As in "stopped obsessing." At least for the moment.

To distract myself, I looked around. We were downtown, next to the Unibank. They have one of those big electronic signs, you know, the kind that tells you what time it is and what the temperature is . . . usually.

Ivy was saying blah, blah, blah, how her dad was some kind of a computer game inventor or something.

I looked at the sign to see how warm it was,

because frankly I was blazing hot under my collar at the horrible sound of Ivy and Mom getting along like the best friends in the world: (Hey, Mom, why don't you just adopt her, if you love her so much?)

I glanced at the sign to see how warm it was outside. I read, instead:

Read your favorite book to your least favorite person—in Pig Latin.

HUH?

I read it again.

Then I quick reached over and poked Ivy in her skinny yet muscular arm. "Ivy! What does that sign say?"

She blinked at me with her mouth hanging open, in mid "charm Nova's mom" stride. The light must have changed, because Mom started rolling slowly forward.

I poked Ivy again and pointed at the sign again. Oh, no! Now it said, "65 degrees, 4:17 PM. Have a happy day."

I rubbed my eyes. It didn't go back to the Pig Latin message.

Maybe Ivy had seen it!

No. She was laughing. Then she said in this totally condescending voice, like she and Mom were the grownups and I was a little kid, "Is your daughter always this weird?"

Mom looked at me in the rear-view mirror, with her eyebrows hiked up to her hairline. "Honey, what's wrong? All it said was sixty-something degrees and the time." She was acting like she was watching purple Pekinese puppies tap-dance out my nostrils or something. "Is it time to make an appointment to get your eyes checked?"

"Sure, Mom," I muttered.

"So, Ivy," Mom said pointedly. "Your dad is a video-game designer? That sounds interesting . . ."

I rolled my eyes and tuned them out. I found myself fingering the charm I always wore on my wrist on a chain. I didn't have to actually see it to know how it looked in the wintry light: a tiny, gleaming silver electric guitar in the shape of a star with a pale green stone on it.

This piece of jewelry was extremely important to me. It was my mystery charm. The one I'd decided I'd actually earned in some weird way by acting on a totally bizarre out-of-the-blue dare. That dare had led me to where I was now: not stuck in ballet, but being my very own individual person. A person who loved to jam with her electric guitar, Roxie, and now with her garage band.

My mind was racing. Had I just seen another of *those* dares? The last one had appeared one day when I was getting some cash out of an ATM machine. This one showed up on a bank sign. Who or what were sending me these crazy messages? Were they some kind of financial voodoo?

Or . . . maybe . . . gasp . . . was I going just a tiny bit insane? Maybe this episode with Ivy had sent me over the edge, and my eyes were playing tricks on me.

But what if it was another dare? I mean, the first one had definitely made my life so-o-o-o much better. My heart beat faster. Did seeing that message on the bank sign mean my life was about to change again? Maybe if I could figure out how to follow it, things would look up in the Joe department?

What a relief when we finally got to Ivy's house. With all these questions running through my head, it felt like the ride had lasted for decades.

"This is it," Ivy said, gesturing at the little shingle-covered house. It crouched behind a huge hedge, like it was hiding from the world. "Kind of like a little hobbit hut, but it's cozy. Private, too—my dad is into that. Anyway, thanks so much for the ride!"

And Mom never seemed to notice that Ivy said not one word to me as she trotted off.

Chapter 4

As soon as I got home, I called my BFF, Yumi. Yumi (it's like "you, me" not like "yummy") always makes me feel better. She's creative. She's fun. She's a good listener. She makes me laugh.

I finished my whole story about Ivy, including how Mom practically acted like she was going to walk Ivy to her door when we reached her hippie-looking house. I mean, wood shingles, tons of stained glass, dangling pots with plants, smoke puffing out the chimney. And that monster hedge in front of it. Okay, so it was actually kind of cute, but Mom didn't have to practically salivate at the sight of it.

"So, then," I went on, "after we dropped her off, Mom talked my ear off about how you and I should have Ivy over sometime when we have a sleepover, that maybe she doesn't have the opportunity to make friends since she's homeschooled. I'm sure she's friend-deficient but it's that poisonous personality of hers!"

"Focus on the bright side!" Yumi said. "You're in a band! This has been your dream for like forever."

"I know . . . But how come my dream had to include her? And why, why, why does she have to like Joe? I mean, I never expected Joe to fall in love with me or anything. But seeing the way she acts around him? It's like torture! I'm not sure I can take it! Do you think I should quit?"

"No! Don't give her the satisfaction," Yumi said. "Besides, you don't know that Joe likes her back. You always say he's the sweetest guy ever. Maybe he's just being nice?"

I took a deep breath. I wanted Yumi to be right. But she hadn't met Poison Ivy. She didn't know just how bad she was. "I don't want to quit. I really don't. But I'm scared I'm going to go totally out of my head if I have to watch Ivy manipulating Joe . . . or in this case 'boy-ipulating' him."

Yes. It's sad, isn't it? Even when I'm in agony, I can't quite stop with the puns in case you haven't noticed.

Yumi cracked up. She's totally my best audience.

I sighed. "I'm caught between two impossible choices. Stay and endure Poison Ivy, or leave and break my own heart."

"Stay!"

I sighed again. "But how?"

"Listen, Nova. This is just like when you had to stand up to your mom. You just gotta stand up to Ivy. Just tell her to back off. It's as simple as that!"

Yumi didn't realize how non-simple it had been for me to stand up to my mom. In fact, if it hadn't been for that bizarre message I saw on the ATM, I'm not sure I would have ever had the courage to try it. Thinking of that made me remember the message I'd seen in the car.

"That reminds me," I blurted out. "I saw something really weird today—"

"Weird, what do you mean?"

But then I started thinking. What if the whole "change your life" thing didn't work if you talked about it? What if Yumi thought I was just plain nuts? Besides, if it was one of those messages, I kind of just wanted to hug it to myself a while.

"Um, I mean, actually it was this weird thing Ivy did. But never mind. I'll tell you about it later."

Yumi and I chatted for a few more minutes about

school, Joe, clothes, Joe, my hair, Joe. We made plans to get together to do homework after dinner, and then Yumi's mom called for her and she had to go.

But I still felt like I wasn't done talking. I was fuming over Ivy, and wondering what I should do. Yumi had helped a little, but sometimes her advice wasn't always a perfect fit for my personality. Just tell Ivy to back off and she will? Maybe for Yumi it would work, but for me? I didn't know.

I had to get a second opinion on my life—like, instantly!

I dialed the number from memory.

Venus was actually studying.

"I can't believe it!" I said. "Studying, of all things! You never needed to, before."

Venus sighed. "I studied more than I let on . . . I was kind of a closet studier in high school, to tell you the truth, Nova."

"What?!"

"Yeah. Confession time. I actually thought it was cool to be the straight-A student no one ever saw crack a book. But I was cracking them, late at night. And now that I'm in Harvard, well . . . I'm just an average student here, little sister."

I gasped theatrically. "Average! Oh, the shame of

it all. I don't know how you can hold your head up knowing that you are just. . . " I lowered my voice to a hush " . . . average. I swear I'll always hold your secret sacred."

"Yeah," Venus said. I could hear the smile in her voice. "Whatever. How're things at home?"

"Oh, the usual. Mom's serving up the green slime. Dad's picking up Roxie and playing some really old oldies—we're talking caveman tunes! But I have no one here to sneak French fries into my room anymore. Boohoo!" I did a little fake-cry.

"I miss you, too, Nova."

Gulp! Instantly, real tears sprang to my eyes.

Weirdly enough, Venus and I hadn't been close at all until right around the time I started making my move away from ballet (to my mom's heartbreak) and toward my own true love, music. Suddenly, my big sis was totally there for me, encouraging me, bringing me junk food feasts in the middle of the night, trying to talk some sense into Mom . . . I mean, Venus was so-o-o supportive.

But after that, we had a month of being best sister buds until she took off for Harvard (at sixteen, with a full scholarship on account of her braininess).

A few times, something's happened and I've been

like, "Just wait until I get home and tell Venus!" and then I remember: She's gone.

"Are you homesick?" I asked. "Aren't you having fun being away at college?"

"It's okay, but I can't help thinking that things will never be quite the same again. And it's just too bad that we didn't start hanging out until so late in our at-home sisterhood."

Man, she really sounded down.

"You'll be home for breaks." I tried to sound cheerful, even though I knew what she was saying was true. Things never would be quite the same. "Maybe I can come visit you sometime?"

"Oh! That would be a blast," Venus said. "But, hey. Enough about me. Didn't you call to tell me something?"

I held my breath. Would Venus take me seriously? After all, a little bit of personality friction in a garage band was small spuds compared to life at Harvard.

Oh, well. I went ahead, and told my big sis my tale of woe.

"Well," Venus said, considering. "That's a tough one, Nova."

I sighed in relief.

"I'm definitely no expert on guys or anything." Yeah.

Like she hasn't had roughly thirty trillion boyfriends and wannabe-her-boyfriends. "You know what I think I'd do?" she went on. "I'd just try to tune out Poison Ivy. I'd throw all my energy into amping up my music skills so I could knock Joe out with my talent. I'd practice like crazy. I'd watch music videos and try to pick up some fancy fingering techniques—and some killer moves!"

"Yeah!" I said. "Fantastic idea."

"Remember what's most important is that you're finally getting a chance to be in a real band. It's your dream! Don't let anything, or anyone—guy or girl—distract you. Go all out. Put everything you've got into achieving your goal. That way, no matter what happens you'll never have regrets. And Nova?"

"Uh huh?"

"Never let go of your dream!"

Wow. I was so pumped up after my pep talk with Venus. She was right. My dream had come true. Sure, it wasn't perfect.

But who was responsible for my happiness? Who could turn it all around? That's right, little old me.

I went directly to my room and started strumming on Roxie. I kept thinking about Venus, and all the good times we had. It's so funny that once I would've given my foot (not either one of my hands! I need them to play the guitar!) to be an only child, and not ever be compared to my gorgeous brainiac older sister. And now I was so sad to have her gone.

My fingers started feeling their way to a bittersweet ballad, and the words to my song appeared in my mind like one of those mysterious messages.

I crooned: "Missing the one you swore you'd never miss . . ."

Chapter 5

All through dinner that night (which consisted of green slime sauté and tofu balls. Can you say yuck?), I looked forward to having Yumi come over to study.

Yumi in person would be just the capper to Venus's speech and the uplifting effect it had on me—kind of like the "two" of a one-two punch to my gloom and doom over Ivy.

FINALLY the doorbell rang.

"I'll get it!" I hollered. When I answered the door, I checked Yumi out. She was as adorable as ever—about as big as a second-grader (although I'd never say that to her). Her hair—about as opposite of mine as you can get—is shiny, gleaming black silk.

She's letting it grow out from the short bob it had been in when I first met her.

Yumi likes to do things with her hair (me, I can only do the very basics with my big wild red curls—braid, ponytail, or bun), and the shortness stymied her creative skills. Kind of like an artist not having paintbrushes, I guess. Yumi is all about being artistic and creative. Usually, she is dressed in some outfit she made out of potholders or refashioned from a thrift-store find or something. That night, she was layered with what looked like a short, casual wedding gown over purple tights. She had on green boots.

She said, "Hey, I'm smuggling a few goodies about my person." She hefted her backpack, which rustled promisingly.

"Thank God!" I said. "I'm starving!"

As per our usual, we scouted rapidly through the kitchen. As per usual, my mom tried to give us some spinach cookies made with wheat germ. (Her idea of a delicious dessert). We passed. But we did let her make us each a big mug of peppermint tea. Despite its healthy reputation, it is pretty tasty, especially with a ton of honey melted into it.

In my room, Yumi opened up her treasure box of tasty delights (otherwise known as her backpack).

"Oh, man!" I said, examining in delight the potato chips, gummy candies, and red-hot jawbreakers she spilled onto my bedspread. "You're the best, Yumi!"

Yumi shrugged. "Hey, no prob. The Suzuki household is one big den of junk-food eaters."

I groped around in my backpack and pulled out my algebra book.

Algebra. I kind of love it, although I wouldn't admit it to anyone. At last, a math for people who like to pretend they're detectives: "Who or what is X?"

"I guess we should get on this, right?" I said. "Have you started it?"

Yumi's eyebrows rose over her glasses frames and nearly disappeared into her hairline.

"Nova!" she said. "What are you doing? We're actually going to do our algebra?"

Our eyes met and we both laughed.

Yumi said sarcastically, "Hey, as long as we're being so academically inclined, maybe I should start reading one of those extra-credit novels. Ms. Neimo would be stunned."

"Did you pick one yet?" I was planning on reading *Jane Eyre*. I'd even checked it out of the library, but I hadn't actually started on it yet.

Yumi swooped over to my bookshelves and plucked out this silly little kids' book. "*Tub Toys*," she read. "This is it!"

I laughed. "Yumi, you're nuts! I think that book has like forty words in the whole thing. Eighty, tops. Ms. Neimo would never give you extra credit for that!"

"She said we could pick any book we want." Yumi cracked open the cover. "Isn't this the one Blue gave you when you quit the library last summer?"

"Yeah," I said. I'd spent most of the last summer volunteering at the library. My library career was topped off when I had to pinch-hit for the story hour reader. Because I'd sung to the kids, I'd actually been a bit of a star, for one brief afternoon. And so the librarian, Blue, gave me this book. Which was very cool.

Yumi laughed and slipped it into my backpack. "Here you go. A little deep reading for whenever you have the time. Your favorite philosophical book."

Which made me think of that bizarre-o message I'd seen on the bank sign. Hey! In a way *Tub Toys* was a "favorite book," right?

I pulled *Tub Toys* back out of my pack and flipped it open to the first page. Blue had written: "Something to read in the tub (and to remember your library friends by!)" All the people I'd worked with at the library had signed it. With an inscription like that, it definitely qualified as a favorite.

I had to try it!

I opened *Tub Toys* and started reading the book to Yumi in Pig Latin:

"Ub-Tay Oys-Tay," I said, and flipped the page. "Addy-day alls-cay out-way, 'Ath-bay ime-tay!' "

Yumi cracked up. By the time I got to the end of the story, we were both rolling on the floor, snorting, hiccupping, crying tears of joy—the works. We made so much noise that my mom came up and said it was time for Yumi to go home.

I wiped the tears away and waved a quick good-bye.

After Yumi left, I shook the book a little, hoping a charm would fall out. I checked under my pillow. I looked under the bed.

No charm.

Of course Yumi did not fit the "least favorite person" description of the message. Maybe that's what was wrong. I slipped the picture book back into my backpack.

Right. I had to look for a "least favorite person." Maybe at school?

If this message was going to change my life, I did NOT want to wait. There was no time like the present, especially if somehow, some way, the message was destined to make Joe like me instead of Ivy.

Chapter 6

A week later, Ivy, Joe, and I were back in Joe's garage for a band session. In between songs and practicing different riffs, we spent a lot of time talking.

"I'm serious about this Band Idol competition," Joe said earnestly. He's so cute when he's serious! He waved a paper in my face. "Check it out! I already picked up an entry form!"

"Cool!" I said. "Let's fill it out right now." I snatched it out of his hand and grabbed a pencil out of my backpack. I sat down on the stage, ready to knock Joe out with how calm and responsible and organized I was.

The first line read:

Your Band's Name: _____

I stared at the paper, stumped. "Guys! What's this band's name? We need one for the form."

Joe looked up from re-tuning his bass. "We never really had one. Even when Roast Beef was here."

"How 'bout we call ourselves 'New Girl and the Real Musicians,'" Ivy said.

I gave her my best fake smile. "Wow. I didn't know you cared."

"Quit joking around, Ivy," Joe said, smiling at Ivy—for just a tiny bit too long. "Let's all think about it. We should just brainstorm wildly."

"Cat Whiskers!" I yelled.

Ivy and Joe stared at me.

"Well, you said to just brainstorm wildly . . . " I could feel my cheeks flush.

"Hey!" Joe put his bass on its rack and pulled an old chalkboard forward from behind a pile of ancient toys. "We could use this! One of you should write down the names we come up with."

"Any volunteers?" Joe said.

Joe and Ivy looked at each other. I mean, they looked at each other. Like, meaningfully.

I cleared my throat, and they reluctantly tore their eyes off each other. Yeah, folks. You're crazy about each other, but—excuse me?—there are other people in the world, too.

I looked at Joe. So cute. My heart burned with pent-up jealousy.

Ivy grinned her mean little smile. "I'm sure New Girl would love to write on the chalkboard. Right, New?"

Yeah. Manipulating me will not work. "That's okay," I said. "You can do it, Old—I mean, Ivy."

"Please?" Joe smiled at me. White (slightly) crooked teeth gleamed like a toothpaste ad.

I sprang up. "My pleasure," I cooed. And I'm not the cooing type. A weird thought passed through my head: Joe brought out unusual traits in me. Could it be that Ivy was actually not so kittenish when she wasn't around Joe?

No—forget it. What a crazy, peculiar thought. Was I totally losing it, or what?

I wrote "Cat Whiskers" on the board.

"Wow," Ivy said, smoothing her sleek cap of pale hair. "That's some wild handwriting you've got going on."

I looked at what I'd written. A little bit scrawly, maybe, but perfectly clear. I erased and reprinted the "k" in Whiskers.

Ivy rolled her eyes. "Oh . . . that's *so* much better."

"Hey, give me a break. I know it's not great," I said. "I'm not used to writing on a chalkboard. But you can read it, right? That's all that counts."

"Are you joking? No one could read that. Your handwriting is just plain gross."

I bristled. Hey, no one has ever complained about my penmanship. It's definitely not pretty and full of curlicues, but it is definitely clear enough to read. I glared at Ivy, who smiled sweetly back.

"I'm just saying," she said. "We've gotta be honest, right?"

Ooooh.

Joe raised his hands in a "time out" gesture. "Nova's penmanship is very cool and original, and definitely worth discussing. But how about if we get back to brainstorming a name for the band?"

Have I mentioned that Joe is the nicest person?

My cheeks heating up in pleasure, I manned—I mean "womaned" the chalk, writing NAME OF OUR BAND at the top of the chalkboard above "Cat Whiskers."

Joe said, "Remember, we're brainstorming. Say anything."

"Garage," I blurted out, and wrote it down.

"Rat's Nest," Ivy said, staring pointedly at my wavy hair.

I shrugged and wrote it down. What*ever.*

"Meow," I said. I wrote it down, without looking at Ivy.

"Rose Between Two Thorns," Joe suggested with a twinkle in his eye. "Or should I say, 'Thorn Between Two Roses'?"

"Gorgeous Guy with At Least One Beautiful Woman," Ivy said.

I sighed. I scribbled.

I looked at Joe. He was smiling at Ivy. She, of *course,* was smiling back.

Such sharp teeth you have, kittycat. All the better to eat you up.

"Green Monster," Ivy said.

I swallowed, hard, and wrote it down. She couldn't mean me. I wasn't jealous. Well, maybe a little bit. Okay, okay. A lot.

On and on we went.

I had a long list when something weird happened.

Ivy suggested, "Garage."

I gritted my teeth. "I already said that one."

She raised her eyebrows. "I don't remember that." Sigh.

I pointed to "Garage," the second word on our list.

Ivy just stared at it. Then she looked at Joe.

He nodded. "Ivy," he said gently, "Nova did say that. It's right there."

And he actually got up and pointed to the word.

"Oh, I see it now!" she purred. "Thanks, Joe."

Grrr. She was so obviously doing this to annoy me.

I fingered my little silver guitar charm, dangling from my bracelet, trying to get a grip.

Hey! Why not?

"Charm?" I said.

Joe shot back, "Three Charms?"

And Ivy said, so sarcastically it would peel the strings off a guitar: "Yeah. How about The Charmed Three? So charming. Not."

Joe and I yelled, "That's it! The Charmed Three!"

We started dancing around like fools, laughing hysterically.

Ivy said, "Are you guys joking?" But then she looked at Joe, at how happy he was, and of course she said, "It's growing on me. Like a fungus. But still. I can live with it."

And so, it was decided. We're now known as "The Charmed Three"!

We settled in to do some riffing. We worked on "Stairway to Heaven," then Joe took off on some finger picking of his own, while I threw in some background riffing. Ivy tried to give us a beat.

Sure, some of it (okay, most of it) was total garbage, but occasionally we'd hit on something that grabbed us.

And for just a few magical moments, I forgot about Poison Ivy, and Joe, and everything, and had the time of my life.

Chapter 7

*I*t's a good thing my Language Arts teacher, Ms. Neimo, is easygoing. I think other, more by-the-book instructors would have definitely done more than just frown at my little performance the next day.

I'd overslept. (I never do that!) I was totally foggy-headed and rushing around, trying to get out of the house fast so I wouldn't be late.

Anyway, I'd completely forgotten that Ms. N. had asked us to find a poem we truly connect with, and then read it out loud to the class. With feeling. Urk.

I suddenly remembered this assignment when she began calling on people and they trotted up, one by one, reading their poems about death and love and food . . . all the big important topics in life.

I panicked! I started furtively groping around in my

pack to find something—anything that would pass as a poem. And that's when I found it. *Tub Toys*, that silly picture book that somehow had gotten into my pack. Hmm, it actually was in rhyme.

No, Nova, forget it. Don't be ridiculous.

But time was passing. Ms. N. would be calling on me any minute.

Carmen Bernstein arose, gracefully scooping her blondish wavy hair behind her shoulders. She began to read a Walt Whitman poem called "Song of the Open Road." Some people are just naturally classy.

When she was done, I came to again. Right. I was in the middle of a situation, here.

Find something else. Get real.

I rummaged fruitlessly through my pack. Nada, nothing, no how.

I could already feel myself blushing—not a promising prelude to having to get up in front of the class, which is something I despise anyway.

Okay, okay, what would Yumi do? I thought.

If I had tons of self-confidence, like her, I'd make up a poem on the spot . . . It couldn't be that hard, right? I searched the room for inspiration.

My eye fell on Jason Shue, across the row from me. In traditional Jason Shue fashion, he was busy carving something into the desktop. (I'm sure he was taking notes on poetry, right? Yeah.) He had his leg out in the aisle, trying to trip people as they walked by, and humming under his breath.

Jase doesn't try and doesn't care. But that's not what bothers me about him. He's got a cruel streak a mile wide. He's a bully with a heart of manure, always picking on smaller kids. Not my favorite person, to say the least.

My eye fell again on *Tub Toys*—

Wait a minute! Wait just a stinking minute!

Tub Toys was one of my fave books. Jase was one of my least fave people (and there might be just a few more in the classroom I wasn't so crazy about).

I could read *Tub Toys* in Pig Latin today in class, ful-filling the message dare *and* my class assignment.

Although . . . Pig Latin? Would it still even count as poetry?

No. Do not go there. Better not to even think about it. Just do it.

And then the fickle finger of fate (a.k.a. Ms. Neimo) pointed toward me. "Nova? You're up."

I am Yumi, I told myself. *I am not afraid.*

"I'm reading today from, uh, well, this book," I showed the class the cover. Some of the slouchers and dreamers sat up a little bit. Jase was too busy with his desk-whittling to even look up.

I carefully didn't look at my teacher. "And," I announced, cheerily, "I'm reading it in a different language."

Everyone's eyebrows lifted. Jaws hung open. And a few people said, "Huh?"

I took a deep breath, just as Yumi would.

"Ub-Tay Oys-Tay," I said, and flipped the page.

"Addy-day alls-cay out-ay, 'Ath-bay ime-tay!' E-thay ob-knay eaks-squay and-ay ater-way ours-pay . . . "

You could have heard a guitar string drop as I read my way through the book. I stumbled a few times—I would have done better if I'd had time to practice! Then again, I would never have done it if I'd had time to practice, because I would have had time to think about it.

When I said, "Ee-thay end-ay," and closed the book, there was dead silence for about twenty years.

And then I heard wild applause and wolf-whistles.

Sure, I got a big kick out of it. But let's face it. The bar is pretty low for entertainment value in school. Anything out of the ordinary qualifies as a big deal.

Unfortunately, the only person not clapping was Ms. Neimo. To understate it, she was not amused.

How did she put it? Oh, yes: "Please do not follow

Ms. Darling's example. I'll see you after class, Nova."

Gulp.

Was I going to end up with detention, or some other sort of cruel and unusual punishment? I have never been the "get in trouble" type. I'm more in the "what's your name again?" category.

But was I worried? Well, some. In the end, though, I was mainly wondering about my charm.

I looked for it everywhere. Was it in my backpack? No. How about my desk? Nope.

I even went up to Jason Shue at the end of class, and gave him the once-over. (He looked nervous.) Would my charm be dangling off his shoelaces, or something?

Where was it?

Hey, if I wasn't getting a charm, then getting in trouble would be so not worth it!

In the end, I totally lucked out. After class, Ms. N. just kind of went on about how she was surprised at me, and how I'd disappointed her by not taking her assignment seriously. But basically she's a nice person and didn't belabor the fact that I'd had a "lapse of judgment." She told me if I did a good write-up on *Jane Eyre*, she'd forget it had even happened.

PHEW.

After school, Yumi and I headed over to Mall-O-Rama, just to check out the guys—I mean "to window-shop." We each bought a cookie at DeLuca's (how could anyone ever resist?) but our friend Bella wasn't working, so we didn't linger.

We strolled through the food court, with its two lines of fast food joints facing each other. It always reminds me of a little old-time village market or something, with people gathered at the tables yakking or standing in line for burgers, pizza, or smoothies. This little village was kind of sunny, thanks to all the skylights, and rather jungly due to all the enormous plants placed hither and thither. And it smelled lovely—like old French fry grease. Then again, I had my scrumptious white chocolate and macadamia nut cookie. Yum.

"Ooo ert," Yumi mumbled. She was not only talking through a mouthful of macadamia nut and white chocolate cookie, but also talking out of the side of her mouth. Like a private eye. Or a gangster.

"Excuse me?"

She started jerking her head around. "Ook ober dere," she mumbled.

"Where?" I asked after translating her garble into "Look over there."

"*Dere!*" What she lacked in clarity, she made up for in volume. Her head jerked again, indicating . . . what?

"Cute boy?" I guessed, my eyes scanning. I didn't see anyone special.

Oh! Wait a minute! I did see someone special. Someone very special. Tall, dark, and hot. Joe. My Joe!

"Let's go say hi," I said to Yumi.

But then I saw her. Her. Who would I be least happy to see sitting with Joe and enjoying a cinnamon roll (which they were actually splitting!)?

You got it. Ivy.

I stopped dead in my tracks.

"Me-ow," I said softly. "Heavy on the 'ow.' "

"Do you still want to go over and say hi?"

I withered Yumi (or tried to—Yumi doesn't wither easily) with one scorching look. I looked back at Joe and Ivy. They had their heads together over a book.

"I guess they're studying together," Yumi said.

"Yeah."

But as we walked away, it hit me. "They can't be studying together, Yumi. She's home-schooled."

And one thing I knew for sure: Joe had never offered to meet me anywhere. Grr.

Chapter 8

*I*vy and Joe didn't act any different the next time we all got together. That is, Ivy was manipulative and Joe was eager to please Ivy.

Like I said, nothing had changed.

But I still felt like a definite third wheel after seeing them together at the mall. Joe was probably reading out loud to Ivy so she wouldn't have to strain her lovely little eyes. Ugh.

Anyway. We practiced, playing some songs Joe had made up. We were terrible. The more songs we played, the worse we got. I started blushing in shame.

Ivy stared at me. "Boy, do we need Roast Beef," she muttered.

I love you, too.

"I think we're just pushing too hard." Joe said. "Let's

take a break. Soda? Water?"

"Oh, Jo-o-o-o-oe," Ivy cooed. "My usual."

He winked (!) at her. "Got it. What about you, Nova?"

"Just a Coke, if you have it, please. Thanks."

Man! I sound like someone's great-aunt with my pleases and my thank-yous.

He went inside with our drink orders.

Q: What do two people say when they're stuck together—and oh, yes, p.s., they happen to hate each other?

A: Not much.

Poison Ivy cleared her throat.

I polished Roxie.

She pulled one knee to her chest and stretched like a sprinter.

I tied my sneakers.

An uncomfortable silence settled in the garage, so thick you could almost see it—like cold gray fog.

I tried not to picture Joe and Ivy bending over the book together at the mall. I know I tend to obsess over things, which has never done me one bit of good.

I won't talk about it.

"I saw you and Joe at the mall," I blurted.

Then I wished I could rewind my life's videotape and erase my words.

"Oh?" Ivy said, casually. "Which day?"

Which day?

"Last week." I tried to sound bored, but I really wanted to scream, *What were you doing? Why were you there together?*

"Oh," Ivy said.

Just that. Nothing more.

The woman knows how to make me crazy. I won't say any more.

"So . . . were you studying?" *Why can't I just shut up? What's wrong with me, anyway?*

"No. I'm home-schooled, remember?"

"Oh, that's right. I remember now."

"What's it to you, New Girl?"

"Nothing. I was just . . . my friend and I . . . "

"You have a friend?"

I bit my lip.

Okay. That's it. Show some class, Nova, for once in your life.

"For your information, I have—" I said, but just then Joe walked in with our drinks. Joe's mom walked in behind him.

"I've got cookies, too," Joe's mom said. "Oatmeal-raisin. Your favorite, Ivy!"

Ivy put on her happy kitty face. "Thanks, Tess."

TESS? Ivy knows Joe's mother so well she calls her by her first name? And Joe's mom knows what kind of cookies Ivy loves? She must be over here all the time. She must be—gulp—like part of the family. Like a daughter-in-law. Double gulp.

Joe's mom offered the plate to me.

"Thanks, Ms. Tsai." Maybe she'd tell me to call her "Tess"? I took a cookie from her plate. "These look delicious."

But I practically had to choke it down over the huge lump in my throat.

When it was just the three of us again, Joe leaned back and crossed his long legs. He was so cute. As always.

Ivy sat down beside him. Way too close.

"Let's talk business here, ladies," he said. "Shall we?"

We nodded.

"I think we're all aware that this isn't working," Joe said. "The question is: why."

"I told you!" Ivy said. "We need Roast Beef back."

Uck. The lump in my throat got bigger. Was Joe

wishing Roast Beef was back too? Now they both wanted to get rid of me!

Joe sighed. "No, I think our problem is that we're trying too hard to pretend Roast Beef is still with us. Instead of playing all the songs we sang with him, I think we need to break out . . . try something new. Maybe we could even find an original song and work it up, just the three of us. I'll bet we'll play better."

Joe turned to look at me. "Nova, you're doing way better than you were with some of those covers—'Do You Believe in Magic' is sounding awesome. But if we're going to go for Band Idol, covers won't be enough. We need something totally unique . . . something that's got that yearning quality. Kind of sad and full of love . . . "

Before I even thought about keeping quiet, I blurted out, "That sounds like the song I just wrote, 'Loving the One.' "

And then I actually, literally, on purpose bit my tongue.

What was wrong with me? Why did I keep blurting things out? Was it my "Blurtday"? Now how was I going to get out of this?

But it was too late. Joe was beaming at me like I was the chicken who laid the golden egg, instead of the girl who laid eggs conversationally speaking.

"All right!" He rubbed his hands together. "We want to hear it, right, Ivy?"

I didn't even look at Ivy. I could feel my cheeks pinking up.

"Oh, never mind," I mumbled. "It's really nothing. I don't think it would be appropriate."

"Appropriate, schmappropriate," Joe said jovially. "Run through it."

"No, that's okay."

Joe hopped up and grabbed Roxie. He handed her to me.

Oh. Boy.

I opened my mouth one more time.

Joe winked at me.

Winked.

At.

Me.

It shut me right up.

He leaned forward expectantly, and I heard my fingers plucking out the chords. I sang, "Missing the one you swore you'd never miss . . . "

My voice sounded whispery and faint at first, but after a bit I forgot I was in Joe's garage instead of my bedroom. I belted it out, crooning the chorus, "Missing, missing, missing you."

When I strummed the last chord, I kind of came to. I didn't know where to look, so I started picking at the calluses on my fingers. Guitar players have calloused hands, in case you didn't know.

But I didn't pick long, because Joe came over and picked me up.

That's right. He picked me up and threw me over his shoulder in a fireman's carry (not exactly the most romantic position on earth—me with my tush in the air).

He ran me around the garage shouting, "The girl's a genius!"

All the blood was rushing to my face (a combination of my position and my embarrassment) so when Joe's mom stuck her head in the garage to ask if everything was okay, and Joe set me down, it felt like my cheeks were on fire. And my hair had poufed up like frizzy cotton candy.

Yeah, I was looking good.

Not.

"Everything's more than okay!" Joe called to his mom. "This red-haired girl you see before your eyes is a talented songwriter."

"Oh, come on," I mumbled.

"Learn to take a compliment," Ivy snapped. "New Girl."

Uh, okay.

Joe stuck a piece of paper and a pen under my nose. "Write the lyrics down for us," he said. "I'll run in and copy them off."

After I scribbled the words down, he quickly ran in and made copies in his mom's home office.

Ivy got all huffy when he handed her one. "Why can't we sing something really good?" she asked. "No offense to you, New Girl..." (Yeah, like I'm believing that) "But this is just sentimental garbage."

Ouch. I felt like I'd been slapped. My eyes stung. I blinked them hard. But I didn't want Ivy to know I cared.

"That's okay," I said, not looking at Ivy. "Just because I wrote this doesn't mean we have to use it. Let's keep searching. We'll find something we all like." My voice shook. I think it was a mixture of rage and oh, yeah, rage.

"Are you guys *joking?*" Joe waved his paper around. "Man, this is totally it. Take my word for it." He looked at Ivy a long moment. "I'll help you memorize the lyrics."

I waited for her to snarl, "I don't need help with the lyrics," but instead she purred, "Oh, Joe, thanks. Maybe we can do it when we meet at the mall tomorrow?"

Grrr. Talk about rubbing it in because you don't get to be the center of attention, for once. Evidently Ivy and Joe had a standing date at the mall. Lovely.

"Yeah, we can go over it some then, too," Joe said off-handedly. "But let's just fool around with it a little bit right now. I'm too excited. I just want to keep playing it, over and over."

Out of the corner of my eye, I watched Ivy drop the piece of paper with my song's lyrics on it on the floor. She stepped on it with her size two high-heeled black leather boots.

Now, don't bother to be subtle, Ivy. Don't mind my feelings.

Things went from bad to very bad in a red-hot hurry.

Joe and I were knocking ourselves out. We were sizzling. However, our drummer kept messing up our tempo. First she played too slow. When Joe (sweetly) pointed out that she should speed up, what happened? You guessed it—she went clear in the other direction— high speed, like a jackhammer operator after drinking two gallons of coffee.

Surely she was tripping me up on purpose.

The fourth time we had to stop, I said, "Ivy, can't you just try to stay with us?"

"New Girl," she said, not very nicely, "why don't *you* stay with *me*? For your information, I'm the drummer. I set the beat."

Joe said, "Nova, I think Ivy will get the tempo perfect with just a little practice. She always has."

Grr. Great. *I can handle this, Joe. I'm capable. Or are you afraid big bad Nova will ruffle the fur on fluffy little Ivy?*

Joe smiled at me apologetically. I guess he could tell I was bent.

He shifted into pep-talk mode. "You know, if we can all learn to work together" (oooh. Anger.) "on Nova's hot song" (oooooooh. Pleasure.) "I honestly think we'll do well at the competition. Then Hawaii here we come for the finals. And if we should win in Hawaii . . . " his voice trailed off dreamily.

Ivy and I looked at each other. Then we looked away, fast. We knew. The winner was guaranteed a contract with a major recording studio. Sometimes bands that were eliminated from the finals were still picked up by studios. It was a way to be recognized, to be discovered.

Joe sighed. "Even if we don't get close to the finals—and I seriously think we've got a shot at that—what's the worst that could happen? We'll have a goal to shoot for. We can only get tighter as a band."

He was quiet a moment, and then he said softly, "Why can't we help each other out instead of accusing each other?" The anger in his quiet voice was more striking than if he had yelled.

I cowered, on the inside.

He looked at me. "Ivy is an excellent drummer, Nova. She's the backbone of the band."

Oh, no! Joe was sick of Ivy and me haggling and, even worse—he totally was taking her side!

My heart sank into my gut. I couldn't even say anything. Would he get rid of me to make his precious drummer happy?

While I was packing Roxie up, all I could think was that I might soon be kissing my life's dream goodbye.

Thanks to Poison Ivy.

Chapter 9

Monday morning, I was at my locker chatting with Yumi, Bella, and Rani.

I wish Yumi and Bella would give a class in how to dress creatively. I could use some tips, and they could definitely teach me some. Bella's hair was all swept to one side (need I say it's straight and silky, unlike the thatch on yours truly's head?) and she was wearing this incredible white eyelet skirt. I looked down at my navy t-shirt and blue jeans and sighed.

"How's the band going?" they asked.

My shoulders sagged. "Let's talk about something else."

Rani gave me a sympathetic look.

"Well, okay," Bella said.

There was a silence while my friends tried to think

of something to cheer me up.

"Have you seen that new movie, 'Crush'?" Rani asked.

"Crush? Is it a wrestling movie? Or something about monster trucks smashing each other?" I said.

Bella giggled. "No! It's a French movie about this girl who has a crush on this guy. It's subtitled, so you have to read along with the movie, but it's such a good romance. Not so racy you couldn't sit through it with a guy. . . not that I did. I saw it with Rani."

"It was cute," Rani said.

"Let's go this afternoon after school, Yumi," I said. "It'll be just the ticket. We'll eat some popcorn, chow on some Hot Tamales or Milk Duds. It's been so long since we've been to a movie."

"Nova, sorry. I can't go. My mom and I are going to this big estate sale preview after school." Yumi and her mom were always finding the coolest stuff at garage sales, flea markets, estate sales, and places like that. Whenever I went along with them, I only saw a bunch of junk, but they had some kind of cool-stuff-radar.

"Maybe tomorrow then?" I said.

"Oh, I think tonight's the last night it's playing," Bella said.

Yumi saw how dejected I looked. "You should go anyway! Eat some Milk Duds for me!"

"No way," I said. "I hate going to the movies alone."

"Have you ever done it?" Rani asked.

"No!"

She laughed. "Me either."

After I got home from school, I felt aimless. My mom and dad would both be at work until five, and it was just me, alone, in that big empty house.

I didn't want to sit there thinking about The Charmed Three, and how it might soon be called "The Charmed Three Minus Me." I didn't want to think about Joe and Poison Ivy, who so obviously were in lo-o-o-o-ve. I didn't want to study. We have no TV, but even if we had, I don't think I would've wanted to watch it.

I fell on my bed, then rolled over and stared at the ceiling. The question was: stay here and have a nice pity party—or find something to do?

It's true. I'd never gone to the movies alone—ever. But maybe it was time to start. That "Crush" movie really did sound good.

After a very brisk bike ride, I treated myself to a giant box of popcorn and a "small" soda (even the small size was enough to keep a tiny country hydrated for a month), telling myself how nice it would be to not have to share them. Too bad I couldn't persuade myself.

There weren't many people in the theater. I slunk into the middle, tossing my coat over the seat nearby. That way, if anyone asked, I could say I was saving a seat for a "friend." I idly watched the commercials the theater played to its captive audience.

(What next? Advertising on your underwear? On the inside of your glasses frames? On toilet paper? Where would it all end? Maybe with ads printed on the inside of your coffin.)

To avoid the commercials (which I sincerely believe can hypnotize you into buying their wares), I looked around at the other people in the audience. A few more had come in. I settled in to one of my favorite passing-the-time activities: making up stories about the people around me.

A very cute older boy sat across the aisle and down two rows. He was in college, I figured, majoring in film-making. Hmm. Now that Joe and Ivy were so obviously an item, I had to move on. This guy shared my love of movies. He'd probably be a famous director someday.

I pictured myself walking down the red carpet on his arm at a movie premiere, with all the paparazzi calling out questions. I'd be wearing a strapless dress. (Hopefully by then I'd have enough chest to actually hold up anything without straps.) Black velvet. And my hair would be subdued, in nice gentle waves with just a few tendrils framing my face.

Yeah, right.

I looked to my right. That older woman with the carefully curled white hair, sitting alone, probably came at the same time every week no matter what movie was showing. Maybe she was all alone in the world. Maybe this was her one true pleasure in life. Was I staring at my own future? Would this be me in fifty years? A lump filled my throat and I sniffed.

Wait a minute! Scratch the lonely little lady thing!

A tall handsome gray-haired man with a small gold hoop in one ear slipped into the seat next to her with a box of popcorn. He slipped one arm around her shoulders. They dipped into the popcorn, giggling and whispering into each other's ears. So much for that.

I twisted to look behind me.

Oh, say it isn't so. Please.

I sank deep into my seat, hoping that Ivy (yes, the one and only Ivy) wouldn't see me as she walked down the aisle with a gray-haired guy who must be her father.

Going to the movies no doubt counted as one of her classes in the "so easy and totally fun" home schooling she was eternally bragging about. I'll bet she'd get an *A* today. I thought of my homework waiting for me and sighed.

Ivy and her dad settled in almost directly in front of me, just a few rows down. Her dad pulled out an apple and crunched into it. The two whispered together like they hadn't seen each other in ten years, never mind spending every day together. Brother.

I braced myself to duck if Ivy turned around to scope out her fellow audience members. I'd have to drop down fast, pretending to tie my shoes. I tightened all my ducking muscles, to be ready for the plunge.

But Ivy didn't turn around. She rat-a-tat-tatted, drum rolling on the arm of her seat (I hoped she was practicing "Missing the One"—maybe she'd actually get the tempo down.)

At last, the lights dimmed, the movie started, and I could relax. It was a romance between a skinny blonde girl and a hunky Asian boy. Hmm. I glanced at Ivy. No wonder she was here.

Okay, I'd try to forget the obvious parallels. Thoughts

about the whole Ivy/Joe thing were what I was trying to escape by being there in the first place!

I consciously tried to lose myself in the story, which had gorgeous scenery and pretty fabulous music. As Bella had said, it was subtitled. As per usual, it took me a few minutes of "I don't want to read this, what a drag" before I was totally into the movie and not even conscious that I was reading.

It was becoming obvious that Ivy and Joe—oops, I mean the movie characters— were *not* going to get together. It was kind of a Romeo and Juliet, star-crossed lovers thing. The two characters were in love, but their families were against it.

I was totally into the movie *except* for one little thing. One tiny little thing, who kept whisper-whisper-whispering to her father. He was whispering back to her, too.

I glanced around. No one seemed to be paying any attention to the whisperers, but I found it distracting and rude. In fact, I kept missing bits of the movie because I was glaring at Ivy and her dad instead of reading the subtitles. When I looked back at the screen, the families were putting pressure on the two characters. The couple were splitting up. Much crying and carrying on. (Okay. So, I had a huge lump in my throat and had to fish for tissues in my jeans pocket. I'll admit it. It was *sad*.)

And then—big drama!

Ivy threw her popcorn box at her dad (popcorn flew everywhere, like a snowstorm) and stomped out. Talk about distracting—couldn't she just turn two thumbs down if she wasn't enjoying the movie? Did she always have to make such a spectacle of herself? What was with her, anyway?

Or . . . ohmygosh. Wait a minute. Maybe all that whispering had something to do with Joe? What if she whispered to her dad to ask how he'd feel if she and Joe got (gulp) engaged, the way the movie people had? And he'd told her that she couldn't. And she'd gotten mad and . . .

No.

I was obviously letting my imagination run away with me. Ivy was probably just trying to get her dad's attention. Maybe she was just bored. Whatever. *I don't care*, I told myself. Ivy was gone. I could settle in and enjoy the movie.

Except I didn't. Couldn't. My concentration was shot for the day.

Finally, I ate the last bite of popcorn and gave it up. I sidled out of the row of seats and headed out into the evening chill. As I unlocked my bike and got situated, I noticed a cap of sleek pale hair shining through a car window, reflecting the street light.

Ivy.

Her face was buried in her hands.

She was crying.

Chapter 10

Naturally, I called Yumi immediately after I reached home.

"And you think she was crying about Joe?" Yumi asked.

"Duh! Of course she was. Don't you get it? The movie was about *them*. Blond skinny girl, hunky Asian guy? And she was whispering to her dad through the whole thing. I'm sure they were arguing about Joe. I think he told her she couldn't see Joe any more. Or even," I swallowed so hard it made a big *glunk* noise into the phone, "maybe he told her she could never marry him. Or something?"

"I don't know, Nova," Yumi said. "Aren't you making some big assumptions? I mean how do you know for sure they were talking about Joe? They could have been arguing about anything. Even if Ivy and Joe like each other, aren't we all a little young for marriage?"

"I guess you're right. It's just that it was really weird." I sighed. "I actually kind of felt bad for her when I saw her crying. She looked heartbroken! But if she wasn't crying over Joe, then what could it be? Do you think her dad's a big jerk? Or maybe she's sad about her mom? She did say her mom died . . . "

Suddenly, a really crazy idea popped into my head. "Yumi! I've got to go to Ivy's house!"

"Huh? I thought you hated Ivy."

"Well, I do . . . But, uh . . . Don't you think I should check on her? Make sure she's okay?"

I stopped for a second, hoping Yumi could read my mind in her usual BFF fashion.

When she said nothing, I said, "Yumi? You're going with me, right?"

"Here, put this on." I handed Yumi my black sweatshirt, as we skulked down Ivy's street. Yes, you heard it right: skulked. (That means "to move in a stealthy or furtive manner," in case you're wondering. Don't feel bad. I didn't know it either until I read it in the introduction to *Jane Eyre*.)

It had taken us about twenty minutes of heavy pedaling to get to Ivy's neighborhood. Then we were afraid to leave our bikes anywhere, especially with it getting dark, so we had to skulk with our bikes.

When Yumi agreed to go with me, I think she thought we were actually going to go up to Ivy's front door and knock. So she was kind of amazed when I gave her my black sweatshirt and made her put the hood up.

"Wait a sec, Nova. Are you saying we're going to spy on Ivy?" Yumi asked, as she pulled the sweatshirt over her head.

"Well, I prefer to use the word—uh, okay the phrase—'subtly check on her.' "

Yumi rolled her eyes. "Yeah. That's good. That makes it not sound as sneaky and underhanded."

I glared at her.

"Okay, okay," she said. "I'm in. I know you'd do the same for me."

When an older man passed us walking the smallest dog I've ever seen on a leash, Yumi and I put our heads together like we were talking about something really important.

"If Ivy walks out the door," Yumi said when the guy had passed us, "she'll be able to see us, you know. We look weird standing here . . . very suspicious. And who knows what the neighbors will think? 'Wild teens looking for trouble' or something. It's getting dark!"

"I know, I know." I looked around. "Let's go down the alley behind her house."

After we had skulked (okay, I know I'm using it too much, but I love that word. Skulk, skulk, skulk. Now it's out of my system) down the alley, we had a clear view into Ivy's kitchen.

The alley itself was very not-scary, just a gravel road with garbage cans behind backyard fences. I was glad Ivy didn't have much of a fence back there—just a short picket fence—so we could see the house. The light was on, so it was like a movie screen in the darkening evening.

Ivy's white hair was hard to miss. She stood at the sink, washing dishes, smiling. She looked like she was humming to herself. Her dad—gray hair, gray beard, a little ponytail—sat at the table with a laptop. I could just make out the glow of the screen.

"She seems okay to me," Yumi whispered. "Let's go!"

Just then, Ivy and her dad turned at the same moment, toward the window. Yumi and I both ducked down.

I held my breath. What was going on? Had they heard us?

Ivy left the kitchen. When she came back, she was with someone tall, dark-haired, and incredibly cute.

Joe!

My heart started thumping away in my chest (not an unusual reaction to the sight of Joe).

Yumi inhaled loudly and made a little nudging motion with her elbow, although I was out of nudging reach.

Ivy and Joe faced Ivy's dad. Ivy's hands were on her hips as she spoke. This looked serious.

Was Joe—oh, please don't make me even think it!—could he be possibly asking for her hand in marriage?

No. Impossible.

But then, Joe got down out of sight. Ohmygosh! Was he getting down on one knee?

He stood up. He handed a paper to Ivy's father. All I could think were two words: "marriage license." Then Joe spoke earnestly, his face serious. Ivy looked from Joe to her dad, Joe to her dad.

Ivy's dad got up. He pointed toward the computer, and talked on and on.

Eh? What's with the computer?

Joe's shoulders sagged. He looked utterly disappointed.

My mouth fell open. Was this what I thought it was?

Yumi and I looked at each other a second. She looked as shocked as I felt.

When I looked back at the window, Ivy and Joe were facing each other. Ivy's dad had sat back down at his laptop. Joe put his arm around Ivy's shoulders and leaned his head against hers for a second.

Then Joe started talking. He stood closer to Ivy's dad. He talked and talked. Toward the end of the speech he was giving (I could hear it now: "Sir, I love your daughter. I'll always make her happy." Cringe!), Joe started smiling.

Ivy's dad was nodding his head slowly up and down. Ivy grinned and clapped her hands together. Then she started dancing up and down and all around.

Oh, man. My stomach tied in knots. It looked like the whole "asking the dad for the daughter's hand" was going better. I couldn't believe this.

Yumi whispered, "Oh, Nova. You must feel awful."

Tears stung my eyes as Ivy's dad stood up and shook Joe's hand. All three were smiling like they'd just won a lifetime of free Ben and Jerry's ice cream. Ivy and her dad embraced. Joe and the dad shook hands again, and Joe patted Ivy on top the head (not the most romantic gesture ever).

As Yumi and I pedaled home, all I kept picturing again and again was the joy on their faces.

"I'm so sorry," Yumi said once we made it back to my house.

I sighed. "That's what I get for spying . . . the worst news I could ever imagine."

Chapter 11

The next day, the usual cast of characters (two of them evidently engaged to be married) gathered in Joe's garage. I'd had a terrible night, reliving the proposal scene and dreading our band get together. I wanted so badly to quit.

But it was The Charmed Three! I had to sacrifice my happiness for the good of the band.

Our practice was going unusually well. Joe showed me a neat slide trick that really added a lot to the song we were working on.

Yes! We had it. We really had it.

Ivy had the tempo. (Finally!) Joe, as always, was giving us the bass. I was singing (and, I hate to admit it, but I totally love my own song).

I was so happy. We were so tight. What a band!

Then, it happened. I actually changed my tempo—I don't know why. Well, I think it was because I lost concentration.

I had turned and caught a glimpse of Ivy's ring finger (nothing) which made me start obsessing over the whole Joe/Ivy/wedding thing again. Would they announce their engagement at the end of practice? You'd think they'd have to tell me sometime, wouldn't they? They couldn't just keep it a secret forever. The more I thought, the slower I played.

I cringed when I realized I was bogging down on the song. Joe had all but told me I'd be out on my ear if I messed up again. I tried to pick the tempo back up, subtly.

"Stop!" Ivy screamed.

Okay, maybe she just said it loudly, but it seemed like a shriek to me. That's what guilt does to you, people. Not to mention fear.

"She slowed it down," Ivy said to Joe. "It sounded terrible. She sounded even worse than usual."

Joe looked at me.

"It wasn't on purpose," I said. I *felt* apologetic and terrified, but I sounded defensive and angry.

"Okay," Joe said. "Well, no problem, then. Everyone makes mistakes, I guess. Let's go again."

You won't believe it. *I* don't believe it. It happened again.

Ivy just stopped drumming and crossed her arms. She said nothing.

Joe raised his eyebrows at me. I shrank internally. Inside, where no one could see, I was about the size of a ping pong ball. That ping pong ball quivered in fear, let me tell you.

Courage, Nova.

I took a big deep breath. "You know," I said. "I actually think it sounds better with the tempo change. It makes it—moodier right there. What do you guys think?"

"Great," Ivy said. "First *I'm* the one throwing us off. And then when you throw us off, it's for the better of the song."

"That song is mine!"

"Yeah, and it sucks. Sentimental, mindless crap."

Tears stung my eyes, but I blinked them away.

Joe raised his hands. "Okay. It's just about time for us to break it off anyway. Let's all think about it with and without the tempo change. We can talk about it tomorrow night."

"Tomorrow?" Ivy and I said together.

"Ladies, we need to amp it up," Joe said. "What do

you think our competitors are doing right now?"

I think Joe is the greatest, but he was going way wacko overboard, being hyper about this competition thing.

Ivy and I looked at each other in sympathy—for all of a millisecond.

"We only have three weeks, you guys!" Joe said, kind of loudly. It made me jump. "We should practice five times this week, or maybe six. It'll have to be after school, but I can't do it at 3:30 on Wednesday, so Wednesday will probably have to be at seven or something. And then . . . "

Huh? "Joe, wait," I said, interrupting him. "Wait, wait, wait! I don't get this. You're making it so complicated! I'll never remember it. Can you write it down so Ivy and I can make copies?"

"Oh, okay. Makes sense." Joe pulled the old chalkboard forward, and held out a piece of chalk. "Nova? Want to do the honors?"

He looked at me.

I just stared back at him. Why should I do all the secretarial chores around here? Who had died and left Ivy queen of all she surveyed? Was it just because she was his uh, "betrothed"? Forget it.

Joe shrugged and started writing dates and times

on the board. "If anyone has any objections to this schedule," he said, "speak now or forever hold your peace."

I looked at the schedule. My heart sank. Sure, I loved to rock out with The Charmed Three (although I'd be a lot happier if it was actually an Ivy-less Charmed Two. Like that was ever going to happen). Yes, I adored being around Joe. Not much made me happier than strumming on Roxie and singing my heart out. Still— Joe's timetable was crazy. Overwhelming.

I snuck a peek at Ivy. She was peeking at me. "Wow," she mouthed.

"Joe," I said, "aren't you afraid we'll burn out at this pace? I mean, I love to get together but we've all got a life, too."

"I think it's better to over-rehearse than to under-rehearse," Joe said. He had a steely, determined look on his face.

Ivy said, "I agree with New Girl." (The first, and probably the last time I'd ever hear *that*, I figured!) "Besides, no amount of practicing is going to help New Girl. She is totally tempo-challenged. Some folks have it." She looked at me, smiled her mean little smile. "And some New Girls don't."

"Thanks a lot."

"Besides, Joe," Ivy went on, "it will interfere with *our* usual plans. We won't be able to get together as much."

Stick the knife in, and then twist it all about, why don't you?

Joe sighed. He sounded genuinely sad (of course, why wouldn't he be, since he was going to miss out on time alone with his *beloved.* Ick.) "I know, Ivy. I'm sorry about it, too. But we need to make some sacrifices. This is important, guys!"

Joe added, "Guys. I don't want to force you to do this. But, would you at least try it? We need to be as tight as possible or we won't even get through the first competition. And we can totally forget about Hawaii."

"Well," Ivy said.

I knew exactly how she felt. It was hard (or maybe impossible) to say no to Joe when he was in the flow.

(Note to self: Write song with these rhyming lyrics! Wow Joe with my genius. Or not.)

"I guess it won't hurt us to try," I said.

"Although," Ivy chimed in, "if I see too much of New Girl, I'm going to regret agreeing to this."

WHAT?!

I whipped my head around and opened my mouth

for a snotty retort, but then I saw that Ivy was laughing like a wicked witch. Why mess with her?

Ivy said, "Do you see any danger of that, Almighty Songstress, So Talented One?"

"Always, So Sarcastic One," I said.

Joe smiled and stretched, all relaxed from getting his way. All oblivious, as usual, to the hatred swooshing through the air like toxic smoke. Did he actually think we were teasing each other? Like friends?

"Tomorrow, then, ladies?"

"Yep," Ivy said.

I kind of sighed out, "Guess so . . . See you guys tomorrow."

Chapter 12

Have you ever heard the saying that goes something like, "Be careful what you wish for, because you might get it?" Well, I'd spent decades of my life (okay, maybe just a few months, but they had *felt* like decades) wishing I could be in a rock band. Then I had a few more wishes—that I could sing and play my guitar constantly. That someone would take my songwriting seriously. That I could hang out with Joe.

Here, all—every single one—of my big life wishes were coming true, and I could kind of see what that saying was getting at!

Hey, don't get me wrong. I did *not* want to go back to taking ballet lessons 24/7 and hiding Roxie in my closet so my mom wouldn't know that all I wanted to do was rock out instead of dance.

But I really had had no clue about how much work the band was going to be. In my daydreams, it had all been effortless. (Then again, in my daydreams I also had perfectly well behaved, beautifully-tendrilled hair!)

The days and evenings rushed by in a hectic blur of sleep (not enough), school (too much), friends (not nearly enough), and band get-togethers (constant).

Ivy and I actually compromised (!!) on the tempo of "Missing the One." The middle-ground beat seemed to suit us both well, as Joe kept pointing out: "We're so tight, ladies! The Charmed Three totally rocks!"

Slowly, slowly, we three totally different personalities were melding into one organism with one mind—at least, while we were jamming.

The rest of the time? Not so much.

Take Wednesday . . . the day I walked in a little late for our session. I stopped short just outside the garage door to gawk at the scene within: Ivy leaning on Joe as he read the song lyrics to "Missing the One" to her. Or was he leaning on her?

I blinked and looked again. Was she actually leaning on him, or was it my perspective? At any rate, she was way too close.

I shook my head in disgust. Why doesn't Joe spoon-feed her meals to her while he's at it?

I stared at my black leather cool-rocker shoes (which I had just bought for cheap at the local thrift store—major score!).

That little voice in my head started yakking at me: Was this aggravation really worth it? For anything? Why didn't I just quit this band and find another one? Any band without Ivy would do.

Then that other little voice that also lives in my brain (must be a duplex!) started arguing with the first one: *Are you joking??? Leave my band? After all the wishing and hoping, my dreams have come true—and now you expect me to leave the band? Over my dead body! I will not skulk on out of here.*

The first voice said: *Oh, yeah?*

Hey, I'm the only person I know who needs a peace-making go-between when she's totally alone!

Joe grinned at me. "Hey, Nova! We're refining, making sure we know every nuance of your sizzling hot song!"

Ivy, looking somewhat less delighted to see me, said flatly, "Hi."

Joe came over to me. I watched to see if Ivy would fall flat without him to prop herself up on.

Nope. Not this time, anyway.

"How're you doing?" Joe asked. "I know I've been

working you guys hard, but we're almost there." He pointed toward his beloved chalkboard, which said, in enormous letters: "Band Idol First Rounds Elimination! Saturday at 3:15 p.m. Civic Center. DON'T FORGET."

I laughed. "Like we could possibly forget!"

And then, in that little lull after I spoke, I heard something. Something terrible. Something disgusting. Something that was such torture to me that I would spill any secret to anyone, any time, in order to stop having to listen to it.

Ivy was humming "The Hampsterdance Song" while she tapped out the rhythm on her snare drum.

AAAAARGH.

My least favorite song in the universe, and the only one guaranteed to instantly go on continuous loop feed through my mind for eternity, messing up my ability to both sing and write songs. Thank you very much. Was there no end to Ivy's evil and underhanded ways? I glared at her.

She hummed on. Louder.

"SHUT UP!" I screamed, screwing up my face and closing my eyes.

You could have heard a guitar string drop. I wanted to disappear. Slowly, I opened my eyes.

Ivy and Joe were staring at me.

"Nova," Joe said. "What's your problem?"

My face was in flames. "Sorry . . . I don't like that song." I swallowed. "It, uh, gets on my nerves."

Joe said, "Well, no kidding." And he wasn't smiling.

He walked over to me. "Listen, I know you're all stressed out. This whole Band Idol thing is a lot of pressure."

I gulped and didn't look at Ivy. "It's not that," I said.

"Then what is it?"

I swallowed again. "Nothing."

Joe sighed.

"I guess we're all used up. Go home and rest."

"So," Ivy said. "What time should we be here tomorrow?"

He looked at Ivy a long moment, and then at me. "I've obviously been driving you guys too hard. I think we'll do better on Saturday if we take the next few days off . . . clear our minds . . . meditate . . . spend a little time apart."

Sure. It was obvious from the way he looked at her. I knew very well what Joe was doing. He was just getting me, the hysterical stress case, out of the way so he could spend time with his beloved, Poison Ivy.

Chapter 13

What an amazing concept: I actually had some time to myself.

Well, other than school and family stuff. But I'd felt so rushed and anxious lately with The Charmed Three getting together every day. Joe, with all his urging to practice and learn and practice and learn and remember, had been upping my weird hyperness to a fever pitch. I can only take so much practice and learning, and then I'm all done, thank you!

I needed some R&R—and fast. It was time to have my BFF for a sleepover.

I'll fast-forward past the good time Yumi and I had on Friday night.

Or maybe I won't, because I had such a blast that I love to remember it.

We dug out my photo album, the one with zillions of pictures of the two of us clowning around, being silly, and otherwise having fun.

Mom (gasp!) actually let us send out for pizza, and she didn't say anything about the pepperoni we ordered on it.

That was the most shocking moment of the night, in spite of the horror movie we tried to watch. We turned it off, finally, not because it was so frightening but because it was so stupid.

BOR-ing.

Yumi said that her main goal for the evening was to make me relax and have a good time and not think about "you know what" the next day.

"What you need is a spa evening," she said.

Uh oh. "Please don't make me over like you did before," I said. "You know I'm not the beautified type. That was a disaster."

Yumi laughed (which didn't exactly comfort me). "Oh, that was just practice! Next time will be much better."

"Uh, Yumi. Hate to break it to you, but there won't be a next time."

Yumi poked me. "Don't be like that, Nova! Sure there will. But tonight we're not doing anything drastic. Just the fun, little girly-girl things. Don't be all worried." Then she brought out the big guns: "You want to look good for Joe, right? Take his mind off little miss who-sie?"

"That's not going to happen." I felt sick to my stomach.

"If you say so . . . !" Yumi said. "How about thinking positive? Oh, and p.s., you'll probably want to look super-good tomorrow anyway." She winked.

"Oh, right. The competition, the one I was trying so hard to forget. Yeah. Thanks, Yumi. Thanks a heap."

"You'll thank me tomorrow." That Yumi. She is so super-confident. What does it feel like to be that way?

We gave each other manicures (every fingernail a different color, thanks to Yumi's huge collection of nail-polish). We put clay masks on our faces.

As I sat there with gunk hardening on my face, I started thinking about how and when my life had gotten so messed up. I was sure that mystery message would fix everything. But so far it'd been a total dud.

Longing filled me. Nothing had ever come from my couple of lame attempts to read my favorite book in Pig Latin. Had that first message been a fluke? Would it ever happen to me again?

I fingered my silver guitar charm. I decided to tell

Yumi all about it (finally), but when I tried to open my mouth—I couldn't! My whole face felt like it was covered in concrete. By the time we'd chipped that off, I was all distracted by Yumi's next beauty plan.

According to an article Yumi read, washing your hair with raw egg is the best thing EVER, especially if you slather it with mayonnaise first. So we gobbed mayo on our hair and let it sit—to condition it.

But something went sadly wrong when I tried to wash my hair with egg. I kept adding eggs because it just didn't feel right. Then, I sudsed it through, and hit it with a lot of hot water. I screamed when I found the first glob. Yumi came running in and screamed too. I actually had scrambled eggs in my hair!

Yumi and I laughed so hard over my three-egg omelet that we rolled around on the floor! That story had a happy ending, but first we had to comb the egg globs out of my hair (and I've got a ton of hair, so it took a while). Then I washed and washed it. The egg and the greasy mayo finally washed out, but I smelled like an egg salad sandwich!

Then things turned serious. I started going off on Ivy and Joe.

"Yumi, what if Joe called off rehearsals so he could spend time alone with Ivy? For the last week, we've been practicing so hard, there's hardly been any free time. You don't think—"

"Nova, quit it! You're being silly. They're probably not as serious as you think," Yumi said, trying to cheer me up. "Maybe it was just a passing fling and now he's over her."

"You saw them that night we, uh . . . "

"Spied on them?"

"I was trying to think of a nicer way to put it." I shook my head. "No, they're really serious. They spend every waking second together!"

Yumi smiled. "You're just exaggerating."

"I'm not! I'll bet you anything if we called Joe's house right now, Ivy would be there."

Yumi's not one to turn down a bet. So we invented an excuse to run down to the neighborhood store. Of course, we knew better than to use one of our phones to make a call when we wished to stay anonymous. Can you say Caller ID?

My hands were sweating so hard I couldn't put the coins in the pay phone. Yumi had to do it. We put the receiver between our heads so we could both listen.

"Hello?" It was Joe!

My heart was pounding out of my chest. What was I doing? Had I gone nuts?

"Hello?" he said again.

And then, in the background I heard something that shocked me even though I'd expected it. It was Ivy's voice calling out, "I brought brownies!"

I fumbled the receiver into the cradle. Yumi and I stared at each other, our eyes wide.

"You heard her?" I whispered.

Yumi nodded.

"So. He was trying to get rid of me so he and Ivy could have a romantic evening. Just as I suspected."

I felt sick to my stomach.

I went to bed that night angry and jealous (I don't recommend that combo for a good night's sleep, by the way).

I lay there, listening to Yumi's slight kitten-like snore. One good side effect of my total snit? It took my mind off the big make-us-or-break-us competition the next evening.

That is, I forgot about it until two in the morning when I woke up, gasping, with my palms wet, and my heart thumping like a bass drum. I'd been dreaming about the competition, and something about Ivy humiliating me in public in front of the judges. And Joe had been on Ivy's side . . .

I slid out of bed, stepping carefully around the

unconscious Yumi/sleeping bag lump on my floor. In the kitchen, I drank a big glass of cold water and pressed my burning forehead to the cool refrigerator door. The urge to crunch something salty overcame me (crunching is such a good stress reliever). I looked without hope into our snack cupboard, full as usual of soy-lecithin cookies, blue algae enriched bars and other baddies—I mean goodies. I could go in and root around in Yumi's stash, currently spread across my desk in all its greasy glory.

"Can't sleep?" Mom blinked at me from the door-way. Her hair was a tangled bird's nest instead of her usual ballerina-perfect bun.

"Sorry, Mom! I thought I was being super-quiet."

Mom sat down at the table. "You were. Believe it or not, I've been lying awake. It was a relief to hear a little mouse skittering around in here, so I had an excuse to get up."

I sat down beside her. She skootched her chair close and put her arm around me. Okay, so I'm fourteen years old and nearly a woman! But, on very rare occa-sions (and I wouldn't admit it to anyone except for you), I need to have the teensiest, most private cuddle with my mom. There is nothing more comforting, not even potato chips.

Mom is a smart (bran and honey) cookie. She knew talking about the next day's competition would only make it worse. So, she blathered on and on, in a soothing comforting voice.

She talked about Venus: would Venus ever decide on a major? She talked about how she and Dad met, but that verged on being too close to guitar talk (my dad played guitar for a band called The Otts in high school) so she left that subject quickly. She talked about her ballet lessons, and how happy she was to be back to them (instead of forcing them on me, I might add. She didn't say it, but I will).

I was so lulled by her chitchat that I actually started confiding in her—in a round-about way.

I said, "Have you ever been in a situation where you liked a guy, but he was totally crazy about someone else?"

Mom gave me a sharp look, and then she got up and made me some hot milk with honey and cinnamon. "Are you talking about yourself?"

"About a friend," I said quickly. "Not Yumi. An . . . acquaintance really."

"Is your acquaintance sure he's not interested in her?"

"It's all too obvious. He wants to be with the

other girl alone all the time. He stands up for her even though she's horrible. And I think—I mean, my friend thinks—she saw him actually proposing to her."

"Sometimes what you—or your friend—sees isn't exactly what's happening. Maybe she's misinterpreting things."

But, listing out all the ways Joe had made it plain that he adored Ivy made me realize with a sickening lurch that there was no way they couldn't be a couple. Even that tiny wishful/optimistic part of me that had hoped I was jumping to the wrong conclusions gave up that night.

Sorrow flooded me, but I felt clear. I would knock them out tomorrow at the competition, and then I'd have to figure out for myself: Stay and watch Ivy and Joe (gulp) marry? Or give up the dream of my life, playing in a band, to avoid my heartbreak?

Just realizing I had no control over Joe and Ivy's relationship—and giving up—made me feel peaceful. All I had to do was get through tomorrow. I sipped my hot milk slowly, feeling comforted and cozy. I started blinking, my lids staying closed longer, longer, and longer.

Just as I was thinking about resting my head on the table, Mom said, "Let me walk you down the hall," and before I knew it, I was waking up to the weak late-morning cloud-dimmed sunshine streaming through my window.

Hooray! I'd made it through the night!

"Want me to hang around?" Yumi asked while we were eating Mom's whole-wheat waffles. Each of those babies weighs about three pounds. They're guaranteed to stick with you for hours, maybe eons. "We could hit Mall-O-Rama," Yumi said.

I shrugged. "That's okay. I won't have much time until I have to leave anyway."

By the time Yumi peddled off toward home, waving to me and carefully not saying, "Good luck, Nova! Call me!" I was ready to get showered, dressed, and head out.

Mom came in to my room just as I was pulling on my baggy blue jeans (the better to dance around in).

"Ready?" She looked at my outfit, complete with plain black T-shirt and my good old thrift-store black boots.

Mom bit her lip. She was no doubt picturing me in my ballerina outfit—the one I ditched when I said "ta ta" to ballet, much to Mom's heartbreak. But to her credit, she didn't say a word.

I grabbed Roxie and my backpack. But when we got

into my parents' old clunker of a car and Mom turned the key, all we heard was an ominous grinding.

"Oh, no," Mom said. Her face had gone white.

"Hey, no worries. It's early," I said reassuringly, trying not to start the stressing-out process. Once I'm in panic mode, it's hard to get out—you know?

After a few more tries, it was obvious the car wasn't going to start.

"I'll call a taxi," Mom said. But she turned even paler when the cab company said it was going to be a thirty-minute wait.

I gritted my teeth. What else could go wrong? No. I refused to have a negative attitude. It was just a tiny glitch in the over-all scene. It would all be fine.

I called Joe, but only got his answering machine. Ditto, Ivy. I was sure the two of them (maybe together??? Aargh, don't think about that! Not now!) were on their way to the competition.

Time was passing. Sure, I was way early. But "way early" was rapidly becoming "a little early" which could turn into "so late that The Charmed Three are eliminated."

"Mom, I'm going to take my bike," I said.

"Your bike? Are you sure? It looks like rain."

Like I had a choice?

I grabbed my pack and my guitar case. "I'll be fine. Don't worry."

"But . . . "

I blew her a kiss. "I'll call you for a ride home afterward, okay?"

And I was out of there.

I passed along blocks of houses, heading for town. Here came the train tracks. I pedaled furiously over the bumps. The tracks were trashed with old bottles and junk everywhere.

Luckily, the Convention Center wasn't all that far away. Especially since I was hauling Roxie and my pack. I felt like an elephant, pedaling and teetering along.

But when my luck runs out and my good fortunes stop, they do it in a big way. I was still a jaunt from my destination, when I

    a. saw the broken glass on the road

    b. could not swerve or stop fast enough due to my arm full of Roxie

    c. suffered an abrupt flat tire

    d. all of the above (Correct Answer! If you chose it, you get an A on this quiz!)

Oh, man. I hopped off my bike (had no choice) as gracefully as that elephant I was talking about.

Now, if I had a cell phone like everyone else in the world, I could call someone. But, no-o-o-o-o, my parents think cell phones are a "needless extravagance."

(Note to self: Tell parents cell phones are safety equipment!)

I snuck a peek at my watch. Sure, I still had some time, but not much.

And, at that very moment, my cycle of doom was completed. ("Cycle of doom" also was a good name for my poor bike, I guess).

The skies opened up. It poured. The wind howled. I felt like I was sloshing around in a washing machine as I hugged Roxie tight, sticking her under my sadly inadequate coat.

Chapter 14

A car pulled to the curb. It looked vaguely familiar to me through the sheets of downpour. As I was trying to figure out who it might be, the door opened and a raincoated figure shouted, "Yo! New Girl!"

It couldn't be.

"I–Ivy?"

"Who else? You look like a drowned rat. Kind of an ugly drowned rat."

Ivy hopped out and grabbed my bike. She stuck it in the backseat of the car.

"What're you doing? That's my bike!"

"I know, dummy. My dad's giving you a ride. So get in, already!"

Oh, gee. It's not like I had any choice at all. I mean, time was passing! And besides, what could I say to Ivy?

"No thanks, I'd rather swim"? But I so-o-o did not want to be in the car with Ivy. Not now. Well, not ever, actually.

"Yo! New Girl!" Ivy swiped the water off her face and stared at me. "Are you getting in, or what?"

I hugged Roxie close. What was I doing? I was going to drown. Better to join the enemy's camp than to dissolve.

"Hi, Nova," Ivy's dad said.

What? He actually knew my name? Ivy didn't call me "New Girl" when she talked about The Charmed Three? He had a weird, big crumpled-up cowboyish hat on his head. And he was way big.

"Hey," I said, settling into the backseat in a huge puddle of my own making. "Uh. Thanks for picking me up. I had a flat tire. And then it started raining. And time was running out."

Ohmygosh, why was I talking on and on and on? I cringed at the sound of my ridiculously jovial voice. I sounded like I was at a party or something.

"No problem," her dad boomed back, when I actually stopped a second for breath. "How are you feeling? Are you nervous? What a big day for you girls!"

"Dad," Ivy said. "I asked you not to talk about that."

Thank you, Ivy.

"Sorry," he muttered. "I forgot."

At the Convention Center, Ivy's dad insisted on carrying both Roxie and my pack in. Then there was a big to-do because he wanted to stay. Poor Ivy!

"Dad," she kept repeating, "it'll be just us and the judges. No audience."

"But I want to support you. I want to be there for you."

"Be there at home," she snapped, finally.

With many loving backward looks (which Ivy pretended she didn't see), her dad took off at last.

"Brother," she muttered. "You're lucky you don't have supportive parents hanging around."

"My mom would've been here," I said, a little defensively. "She's totally supportive."

Ivy laughed shortly. "I guess you didn't hear. I said: 'You're lucky . . . ' !"

I had to laugh, too. "Gotcha."

Okay. So I was having slightly warm fuzzy feelings toward the evil Poison Ivy. Maybe it was because we were heading off to battle together. Don't enemy soldiers bond in the face of horrible fear?

Ivy squinted at the Band Idol sign posted in the lobby.

I read the sign over her shoulder. "Looks like we need to go to the third floor. There's a waiting room there, where we hang out until we're called." Gulp. *I will not think about it. I will just do this.*

I scoped out the seemingly empty lobby. Was Joe already upstairs? Knowing him, he'd been there for hours, making friends with the other bands.

"I wonder where Joe is?" Ivy said.

"You don't know?" I shrugged, as if Joe had never crossed my mind. "I'm sure he'll get here," I said airily.

I stepped on. "Let's go, shall we?"

Ivy pressed the third floor button, and the doors closed. All of a sudden, I couldn't avoid thinking about where we were headed, and what it meant. A lightning-quick thought flashed through my brain: *Will I even remember how to play Roxie? Will I forget the words to my own song?*

An uncomfortable silence filled the small, moving room. The elevator was shabby, with peeling tacky red and gold flocked wallpaper. It shuddered as we moved, and then it made a weird grinding sound. It smelled musty, like an old house that hadn't had its windows opened in ten years.

I looked at Ivy. She looked at me. We both cleared our throats.

Thank goodness it's only for a minute.

But it wasn't. Because just then, the elevator clanked. It stopped. Jerked. Froze.

For good. Maybe forever.

Yes. This was my life—and so of course I would be trapped for eternity in a dinky elevator with the person I most despised in the entire world. How else could it be for the least lucky person in the entire universe?

I closed my eyes and fought my panic, trying to slow my breathing into something that resembled respiration instead of a fireplace bellows pumped by someone who's had twenty lattes.

I sat down on my pack and gently settled Roxie next to me while Ivy calmly pressed the emergency button.

"Press it hard," I couldn't help saying. "Press it over and over."

"I believe I know how to press an elevator button," she said, pressing hard and repeatedly. "Quit being so panicky."

"Uh, Ivy. Shouldn't we be able to hear the alarm bell ringing when you press the button? I don't hear a thing."

Not to rain on your optimism parade.

She frowned. "I don't know." She pressed it again. "I don't hear anything either. Maybe it rings somewhere else, like in the maintenance department."

"We can only hope."

Ivy glared at me. "You always see the worst in any situation, don't you?"

I opened my mouth. Closed it. What was the use?

I found myself literally gnashing my teeth. We would never get to the third floor waiting area. They'd call "The Charmed Three, please!" and Joe would have to say, "I'm sorry. My band members flaked out totally."

"Joe is going to hate us," I blurted.

"No he won't." Ivy crossed her arms. "If you knew him like I do, you'd realize he won't hold it against us."

Grr. Why didn't Ivy rub it in a little bit? So she knew Joe better than I did, so what? Like I cared.

Okay, I did care—big time. But now was not the time for Joe one-upmanship. Any fool, even Ivy, should be able to see that. We were in the middle of a true-life emergency.

She was inappropriate. So why did it bug me so?

"What ev," I said, trying for flippancy instead of flip-off-ancy. "We've got better things to worry about right now."

(Although I was actually the one to bring Joe up . . . hmm . . .)

"Let's stay calm," I panted.

I sprang at the elevator door, beating it like I was a champion boxer facing my worst opponent. *Wham, wham, wham!*

"Let us out!" I screamed. "We're trapped in here! Help! Help!"

Nothing. Nothing but a pounding heart, a headache that could split granite, and a terrible fear of looking at my elevator-mate. She must be appalled at New Girl's out of control rampage. She, at the very least, would be chortling, meanly.

I felt her pinch my arm. Hard.

"Chill, New Girl! I think we're going to be in here for a while."

I looked at Ivy, who was smoothing her already-smooth hair down. She sank gracefully into a cross-legged pose.

And then she started singing.

Oh, no.

It couldn't be.

Yes, it was. "The Hampsterdance Song."

I clapped my hands over my ears, but it was too late. That tune, that horrible, horrible, disgusting song seeped into my poor brain.

But that was her business, right? After all, as Venus

always says, you can't control what others do. You can only control how you react to what other people do (get it? Try to keep up, now). And I would react with dignity. That's right. I was done griping about things. I would complain and whine no more.

Ivy sang softly, "Da dit de doh . . . "

"Ivy!" I whispered. Okay, I said. Well, to tell the truth, I shrieked is probably more like it.

She stopped singing. "What?"

"That song truly makes me crazy. Remember? I told you guys that! It's why I totally lost it at our last session. It sticks in my head, and it's all I can think about. I can't play the guitar. I can't remember lyrics. It ruins me, it absolutely ruins me." I knew I was being a drama queen, but I didn't even care. "So quit it! Please!"

Ivy stared at me with her mouth open. " 'The Hampsterdance Song?' You hate it? I thought you were just freaking out."

"I was freaking out because I detest it! Doesn't everyone?"

Ivy shook her head slowly. "It's my favorite song. I always hum it when I'm stressed out." She stared at me. "Wow. Who would've thought it?"

"Well, now you know."

I stared at the ceiling. "Do you think I could climb out that trap door up there?"

"And then what?" Ivy said. "Are you going to shimmy up the elevator shaft? What if they fix it and move the elevator in the meantime? It could actually squash you."

Sigh. She had a point. I sat down.

Ivy rooted around in her coat pocket. "I'll share this candy bar with you, if you'll quit acting hysterical. Want some?"

My stomach growled. "You bet I do."

We sat there, Poison Ivy and I, eating the candy in teensy-tiny bites to make it last.

"Thanks," I said, when I'd licked the last molecule of chocolate off the paper.

I was still hungry, though. Maybe I had something to share?—some little munchie from Yumi. An apple, even old and withered, would taste fine. I could eat anything! Even a made-by-Mom soy/lecithin/bran treat!

Rummaging around in my pack, I found a stick of sugarless gum. Rats! I pulled it out, and a book fell in my lap. *Tub Toys*, that picture book of mine. Looking at it, at the bright weird/silly picture on the cover and having Ivy near me made synapses connect in my brain or something.

All of a sudden, I was thinking about that crazy

message I'd seen on the bank sign, with Ivy sitting next to me in the backseat. *Read your favorite book to your least favorite person—in Pig Latin.*

Gee, and here I was with my least favorite person, with nothing to do. What a coincidence. Plus it might serve to take my mind off my horrendous situation, for at least five minutes.

"Look." I showed the book to Ivy.

Ivy frowned at it. "What's it about?"

Duh. I gestured at the title. "Tub toys. Obviously." I laughed a little bit to soften my snottiness. I am really not a "mean girl." But sometimes I'm an "irritated girl."

"Are you going to read that to me?"

Okay. As you know, I had been planning on reading it to Ivy.

Q: So why did it bend me out of shape to hear her ask that?

A: Because I'd heard it from her so many times before, either to me or to Joe.

I sighed. "Ivy, it would be my pleasure to read it to you—in a foreign language!"

I cut her "HUH?" short by saying, "Ub-Tay Oys-Tay." I flipped to the first page.

"Addy-day alls-cay out-ay, 'Ath-bay ime-tay!' E-thay ob-knay eaks-squay and-ay ater-way ours-pay . . . "

You think reading something in pig latin is easy? Try it sometime. Sure, it was minutely smoother than I'd been reading it in class. I guess that tiny bit of practice helped. Plus, I didn't have the knowledge that a bunch of students and a teacher were listening. Still, it took me a while to get to "Ee-thay end-day."

I looked up. Ivy was frowning at me and looking at the words. She looked totally bewildered!

"Nova," she said hesitantly. "Would you mind reading it to me again?"

"Why not? We're not going anywhere."

I stumbled my way through *Tub Toys* again. And then again. By the fourth reading, I had the whole book memorized in Pig Latin! (I'll bet not many people can say that!)

I could feel each second dragging by like it was an eon.

I stared at the door. "How long have we been in here?" My heart began thumping.

"Not that long . . . cool it, for crying out loud."

I closed my eyes.

"New Girl?"

I kept my eyes closed.

"Uh huh?"

She was quiet so long that I peeked at her. She was staring at *Tub Toys*, which was lying on my pack. She picked it up and opened it.

"Where did you get this?" she asked. "I've never heard of a book written in Pig Latin before."

I laughed. Oh, brother. "Of course it's not written in Pig Latin," I said. "I just read it that way."

And.

Then.

It.

Hit.

Me.

Like a flurry of scenes from a movie, I heard Ivy asking Joe and me, over and over, to read something to her. I saw Ivy squinting at the bank sign without answering, after I asked her to read it to me. I saw Ivy refusing to write on the chalkboard, and Ivy squinting at the sign in the lobby.

I stared at her, my mouth hanging open.

"You know I can't read, right?" Ivy said softly. Hesitantly, like she was afraid I'd make fun of her. "Well, I can read a little bit. But, not much."

"Actually," I said, when I recovered my voice, "I just now realized it."

"Oh. Well, yeah. I'm just now learning. I've got a tutor."

"Oh?"

"Joe. Joe tutors me. We meet at Mall-O-Rama food court and the library and sometimes after you leave practice."

I blinked at her. Would wonders never cease, here?

"He is so into reading! My dad offered to pay him, but he refuses. He says he just wants me to feel what a joy it is to get into a book."

"But . . . " I said. "Don't you love . . . well, I mean 'like' Joe? Aren't the two of you a couple?"

Ivy laughed. "Joe and me? You've got to be kidding. No way! He's like my brother."

I must have looked really relieved because Ivy lifted one eyebrow. "Wa-a-a-it a minute," she said slowly. "You? You like Joe."

I bit my lip. I swallowed hard. I nodded. "But . . . "

"Hey, don't worry. I won't tell him."

Whew.

"So if you don't like Joe," I said, "why were you acting like you owned him? And you keep being so brutally mean to me!"

"Oh. That."

I waited.

Ivy stared at her hands. "The way Joe talks about you, I figured he was going to start hanging out with you. Then bye-bye, Ivy's reading lessons!" Ivy stared at the floor. "Well, also. I didn't want Joe to like having you in the band. I really wanted him to convince Roast Beef to come back."

"What's so great about this Roast Beef guy anyway?"

Ivy shrugged. She had a funny little smile on her face. "He's just really cool . . . "

I stared at her. "You have a crush on Roast Beef!"

Ivy looked sheepish. "Promise you won't tell Joe? I would die of embarrassment!"

"Don't worry. If you don't tell Joe about my crush, I won't tell about yours!"

We both laughed. And then I thought of something else. "Ivy, I saw you at the movies the day you ran out of the theater. And then I saw you afterward."

She looked at me.

"You were crying in the car," I said.

"Well, how would *you* feel if you couldn't make head or tails out of a movie because you couldn't read the subtitles?"

I felt like an idiot. Of course. "There's one thing I don't get, though. How is it that you've never learned to read?"

"I've got a learning disability, I guess." Ivy shrugged, but her voice shook a little bit. "It's not so bad. I guess it would have been caught earlier if I was in regular school. But my dad is such a 'whatever' kind of a teacher. He figured I just wasn't ready. He never pushed me." Her voice dropped to a whisper. "Maybe it would have been better if I'd been pushed along a little bit."

"Oh."

"I'd been trying to talk my dad into getting me some help, and getting me into your school. But he thinks public schools are evil, and he suspects anyone who works for them."

"Huh?"

"Yeah, well." Ivy looked down. "He's kind of a nut about some things. He's one of these conspiracy theory guys. He doesn't trust any institutions like schools and banks and post offices and stuff. It's crazy, I know. But other than those things, he's a great guy. Seriously." She smiled. "In fact, just the other day, Joe finally persuaded Dad to get me some real help. He came over to my house and explained everything. So now I've got an appointment with a reading specialist. I am so stoked!"

Oh, man. The scene in Ivy's kitchen flashed before my eyes. The paper Joe handed her dad must have been information about the reading specialist.

I felt so-o-o bad about all the thoughts I'd had toward Ivy. She wasn't a user. She wasn't lazy. She wasn't even Poison Ivy. She just couldn't read, and she probably was defensive about it (who could blame her?), which explained her major attitude. Not to mention living with a conspiracy theorist. Yikes. Who would've dreamed it?

"Oh, Ivy," I said. "I don't even know what to say."

"You don't have to say anything," she said. "You know what my fantasy is? My big dream is to go to your high school. But, natch, I can't do it if I can't read. Can you imagine? So, that's my goal in life."

"I'd be happy to help," I said. "I know you've got Joe, but . . . "

Ivy laughed. She wrapped an arm around my shoulders and gave me a squeeze. That girl's got muscles, let me tell you! She's got one powerful hug.

"Hey, New Girl. I can use all the help I can get," she said. "Even from you."

We smiled at each other. Like band mates. Like friends.

"Speaking of 'help'," Ivy said. "Maybe we should scream our heads off. Want to try it?"

I discovered a new talent in myself that day. Not only could I admit to myself that I was totally and completely off base about someone, but I could scream like you would not believe.

Ivy looked at me, shocked, after our first duet of "help, help, HELP, HELP!"

"Wow, do you have lungs," she said in admiration.

"It's gotta be all that singing," I said modestly.

And finally, finally, we heard a man's voice calling, "Hang on! You'll be out of there in a minute!"

The elevator moved slowly up to the next floor.

When the doors opened, a man in navy blue work clothes stood there, shaking his head. He slapped a big OUT OF ORDER sign on the door. "You girls okay?"

Ivy and I hugged each other. "We're fine!" we said.

But we were more than fine. We were free.

Chapter 15

"Y ou're here!" Joe shouted, running to us and gathering us both into one huge hug. "They just called us."

I had no time to look around at the others hanging out in the waiting room. I had no time to pee. I had no time to shake out the rock that had suddenly appeared in my boot. (How does that happen, anyway?)

We, The Charmed Three, just marched on into the room.

In one glance, I could see that it looked like a school auditorium, with a stage and row upon row of folding metal chairs. It echoed while we set up on the stage.

Then we climbed down the stairs (my knees were trembling) to speak with the judges, seated in the front row with pads of paper. One of the judges, a big guy with a walrus mustache and round glasses that reflected the light so we couldn't see his eyes, gave us the scoop, sounding as serious as if he were prepping us to perform brain surgery.

"You'll sing one song," he said. "Then wait in the adjoining room. We'll announce the winner at seven, when the bands will file in here individually in the order they played. You're number thirteen by the way."

"Thirteen?!" I heard Joe groan.

"My lucky number," Ivy and I said at the same time.

We giggled. Nervously.

When we climbed the steps and I picked up Roxie, I thought I'd die from nervousness. Even my breathing was shaky, and Roxie slipped in my wet palms. I almost dropped her.

However, as soon as I had Roxie tuned, and Joe said, "Are you ready?" I was. I turned to look at my bandmates, and (not to get all new-agey) a peaceful spirit seemed to settle us, joining us. We smiled at each other. This was it.

I know it's bragging, but I've still got to say it: We were on fire. I lost myself in "Missing the One," and it felt like being in my homeland. The Charmed Three played like we were charmed.

What could explain our performance that day? Was it the new friendship budding between us? Was it some kind of vibe Ivy and I had picked up from each other from being so near to each other for so long? Or relief that we were free?

There was a little silence after we finished. Joe, Ivy, and I looked at each other, all flushed and radiant and glowing.

What happened then was truly unbelievable. One of the judges, someone who hadn't even made an impression on me, a short round guy with black mutton-chop sideburns (why do bald guys so often go for big facial hair?) actually applauded.

Gee. I didn't know if we should bow or what. I got all flustered, stumbled around, and almost fell off the stage. Joe grabbed my arm, kind of casually like he was in the habit of hanging on to me. (To clue you in on how nervous I was, it hardly registered.)

"Easy," he whispered, out of the side of his mouth, like he was calming a horse.

The other judges were blank-faced, but Mr. Mutton Chops beamed like he'd just been given a check for a billion dollars. You had to love it.

"We'll start calling each band in at seven," another judge said. Now, her I noticed—must have been the ten thousand tiny navy blue braids all over her head. Kind of a major fashion "don't" at a certain age (not like I know fashion. But still.) She had her many-braided head down and was writing like crazy on a piece of paper. I tried to see what she was writing, but couldn't.

"Thank you," Joe said as we filed past.

Ivy and I echoed his thanks.

"My knees are shaking," I whispered when we were back in the waiting area.

"Me too!" Ivy squealed. "Wasn't it awesome, though? I was so into the music, I didn't even know what planet I was on!"

"Same here," Joe and I said.

We had only an hour to wait for the verdict. I say "only an hour" lightly, but it was an hour that lasted about a million years.

By mutual consent, the three of us went to separate corners of the room. Joe read *Lord of the Rings*. I looked at Ivy, sitting with her eyes closed across the space that looked like a big doctor's waiting room. I obsessed about the judge who loved us vs. the ones who appeared to have absolutely zero reaction to our stunning performance.

Did the sideburn guy clap for every band?

Were we so bad that he felt he had to cheer us

up? Kind of like giving a kid who's fallen off his bike a lollipop? His appreciation had seemed genuine, but the more I thought about it, the more sarcastic it might have been.

I wiggled my foot around in my boot. What was in there, anyway? I pulled the boot off. A tiny silver book clattered onto the linoleum floor. I snatched it up.

My charm! I looked it over, running my fingers over the slick cover of the little silver book.

I clutched it and looked at Ivy. Reading to her in Pig Latin had opened the cover on her life's story. Ivy would always be Ivy—she definitely had an edge. No doubt she'd continue to grate on my nerves at times. Nevertheless, I knew we were going to be friends from now on.

I started smiling. I clipped the charm onto my bracelet, right next to my lucky guitar charm.

I closed my eyes just for a second.

"New Girl! Wake up!" It was Ivy, and for one instant I automatically disliked her by force of habit.

And then I remembered. Oh. Right. We weren't enemies any more. What a load off my mind not to have to go around practically hating someone!

My hand went to my pocket. Had I dreamed the charm? No, there it was!

"Nice book," Ivy said.

I gasped. How did she know about my charm? But then I saw that she was pointing at my knee where a leather book lay. It had a velvety dark gray cover with a shiny silver star embossed on the front.

Oh!

I knew even before I flipped the pages that they were blank.

"Thanks," I said, settling it into my backpack.

I gave my brand new buddy a great big goofy grin. "Hey, there, Ivy!"

She tugged at my hand. "Come on, New Girl! They called our name!"

Huh? Oh. Right. The competition.

THE COMPETITION!!!!!

We filed back into the main room, and the judges pointed at a small group of straight-backed chairs.

We sat down. I forgot to breathe for a while. Across a shiny dark wooden table the size of Siberia, the judges shuffled papers around, whispered, and smiled slightly. It was impossible to tell, though, if those were "you guys are winners" smiles or "I'm sorry for you guys" sympathy grins.

Will you say something please? Are you enjoying torturing us, or what?

I couldn't bear this. I couldn't take the suspense. I couldn't stand to look at these people who were deciding our fate. I couldn't look at the other members of The Charmed Three. I rubbed my new book charm with my sweaty fingers.

Come on. I mean, I knew I was in the real world. I was sure we wouldn't actually win but maybe one of the judges would be impressed enough with what we'd done, and have some connections . . . my mind floated off into fantasyland.

"Aloha, winners . . . " said Ms. Blue-Braid.

I kind of went blank there for a second. Words and phrases whizzed through the air. I caught some of them: "best performance," "good luck in Honolulu," "remarkable," "reporters waiting," and "stars."

And then it hit me like a ton of bricks. I sprang up. Ivy and I gave each other a quick hug, and then Joe got in on it. Group hugs—kinda weird, I guess. Unless you're with two of your friends, and you've just shared an amazing experience.

The winning of the contest, huge as it was, was the second best thing that had happened to me that day. I lifted my wrist and stared at my new charm.

How lucky could one person be? I'd had another mysterious message, which had given me another friend.

I caught Ivy's eye, and we beamed at each other.

Then I noticed Joe had taken out a notebook and was taking notes. I was sure he was writing down dates and other important info in his usual gung-ho fashion.

I reached into my backpack and took out my new journal, along with a pen. I had important notes to make, too, after all.

Two ordinary girls
Two mysterious messages
Two crazy dares

Nova Rocks!

Nova secretly dreams of being a rock star. Her mom insists she take ballet. Will a mystery message help Nova follow her own dreams without breaking her mom's heart?

Carmen Dives In

Carmen's step-sister Riley is a super cheerleader, world-class diver, and all-around perfect person. Carmen wants to hate her. But when she follows her mystery message, she discovers there may be more to Riley than meets the eye.

Do a dare, earn a charm, change your life!

Ask for Star Sisterz books at your favorite bookstore!

For more information visit www.mirrorstonebooks.com

For Bella and Rani life will never be ordinary again!

Bright Lights for Bella

Bella gets cast as the lead fairy in the school play. There's one problem: she's scared of heights! Will the mystery message help Bella overcome her fear before she soars over the stage?

Rani and the Fashion Divas

Rani longs to be part of the Fashion Divas, the most popular girls in school. But when she follows the mystery message, she finds something she never expected: a true friend.

Do a dare, earn a charm, change your life!

Ask for Star Sisterz books at your favorite bookstore!

For more information visit www.mirrorstonebooks.com

EXPLORE THE MYSTERIES OF CURSTON WITH KELLACH, DRISKOLL AND MOYRA

THE SILVER SPELL

Kellach and Driskoll's mother, missing for five years, miraculously comes home. Is it a dream come true? Or is it a nightmare?

KEY TO THE GRIFFON'S LAIR

Will the Knights unlock the hidden crypt before Curston crumbles?

CURSE OF THE LOST GROVE

The Knights spend a night at the Lost Grove Inn. Can they discover the truth behind the inn's curse before it discovers them?

**Ask for KNIGHTS OF THE SILVER DRAGON books
at your favorite bookstore!**

For ages eight to twelve

For more information visit www.mirrorstonebooks.com

MORE ADVENTURES FOR THE

FIGURE IN THE FROST

A cold snap hits Curston and a mysterious stranger holds the key to the town's survival. But first he wants something…from Moyra. Will Moyra sacrifice her secret to save the town?

DAGGER OF DOOM

When Kellach discovers a dagger of doom with his own name burned in the blade, it seems certain someone wants him dead. But who?

THE HIDDEN DRAGON

The Knights must find the silver dragon who gave their order its name. Can they make it to the dragon's lair alive?

Ask for KNIGHTS OF THE SILVER DRAGON books at your favorite bookstore!

For ages eight to twelve

For more information visit www.mirrorstonebooks.com